PLAY FOR TIME

A WITCH IN TIME: VEE BOOK 2

STEPHANIE DAMORE

ONE

"I don't know, guys. Maybe we're moving too fast," I said to my friends on the phone. Michael and I had spent Halloween together, not to mention solving <u>that crazy Christmas curse</u>, plus dozens of dates in between, and now this.

"Wait, what? Where is this coming from? You're crazy about Michael. And it's a weekend getaway for a wedding. It's not like he's putting a ring on your finger," said Lexi, my best friend and fellow time-traveling witch.

Lexi had a point. We were going away for a wedding, but not ours. Michael's friend was getting married in Chicago in nineteen sixty-two, the year my boyfriend was from, and he asked me to be his date. The groom was a warlock, the bride a shifter, and Michael was the best man. At the time, a supernatural wedding sounded like a blast, but now I had cold feet, hence the conference call to my witch-in-time colleagues and confidants.

"True, but I'd be suspicious. How well do you really know him?" chimed in Mariana on the other line.

"Well, we've been dating for six months." I found myself switching sides and defending my relationship.

"I say trust your instincts," weighed in Nuala.

What were my instincts saying? I thought for a second. Michael just wanted to go away for the weekend with his girlfriend. Nothing more, nothing less. I needed to chill out, and yet I couldn't. I was breaking all the rules dating Michael.

Whose rules, you might ask?

Well, mine.

I never dated warlocks, and I never, ever fell in love with them. It scared the bejeezus out of me that my relationship with Michael was heading into uncharted territory.

I thought about the wedding. My heart fluttered in anticipation at the thought of seeing Michael in a tux standing at the altar. Good gravy. When did I start having so many feelings for the guy? I visibly gulped. I'd give anything for the Agency to send me off on a cold case right now and buy me some time to think. I'd love to take a couple of days, go back to 1980, and solve a mystery, even though I had just gotten back from a case. I looked around in desperation for the unscripted delivery box from the Agency of Paranormal Peculiarities that would often magically appear, but the only thing I saw was Agatha, my feline familiar, snoozing on the back of the couch.

"Besides, if he hurts you, we'll curse him a hundred different ways," Nuala added helpfully. That got a smile out of me and reminded me why I loved these girls so much.

There was a knock on the front door. "Shoot, guys. I gotta go."

"Have fun! It'll be fine," Lexi said.

"If it's not, you know where to find us," Nuala added.

I clicked off with the crew and took a second to smooth out my outfit and check my reflection in the hallway mirror. The dress was vintage, my hair platinum, and my expression anxious. My magical powers fed off my nerves in response. I could feel the electricity humming through my veins, causing my fingertips to tingle.

I took a calming breath, plastered a mega-watt smile on my face, and opened the door to greet my guy.

"Hello, beautiful," Michael said.

"Hello, yourself," I replied, eyeing Michael appreciatively. He wore navy slacks with a black belt and a white button-down dress shirt. A dark-gray trilby hat topped off the look. "Sorry, that was lame," I said, shaking my head and realizing I sounded like a dork.

Michael removed his hat and bent to kiss my cheek. The moment his lips made contact, it was magic. Literally, an electrical current flowed from my body and zapped Michael's lips.

"Hey!" Michael jumped back, rubbing his hand on his mouth and then smacking his lips together as if they were numb.

"Sorry!" I jumped back too and touched my cheek. It had been a long time since we'd shocked one another.

"Everything okay?" Michael eyed me with concern.

"What? Yeah. Absolutely. It's been a crazy week with work, that's all. I'm definitely ready for some downtime," I lied, holding the door open for Michael to come inside. I closed the door behind him, pausing to close my eyes and take a deep breath to calm myself down.

"Afternoon, Agatha," Michael said to my familiar.

I turned and caught Agatha mid-yawn. She stared at Michael for a beat before closing her eyes and returning to her catnap without so much as a hello.

I shook my head. Unless you had a bag full of kibble or a can of tuna fish, Agatha couldn't be bothered. Agatha liked being a cat, and who could blame her? Her life was full of lazy days sleeping in patches of sunlight and wild nights chasing shadows up walls. If I get a chance to be a familiar, I'll probably pick the feline form too. Although, I'd want to tag along with my witch on cases, unlike some cats I know. I eyed Agatha. She had no idea I was even thinking about her.

"You ready?" Michael asked.

"Almost. Just give me a minute," I lied once more. The truth was, I hadn't packed a thing. I had just gotten back the night before from a cold case in 1995, and before that, it was 1972. A mixture of clothing from two decades lay about my floor. Stonewashed jeans and a flip-open cellphone clashed with a tie-dye dress and bell bottoms. Make that three decades if I counted the pleated skirts and coordinated gloves, hats, and heels I wore for my dates with Michael back in the sixties.

I hurried up the old farmhouse's wooden staircase and disappeared into my bedroom. The suitcase sat open on my bed. I did a circle about the room. It's tricky vacationing back in time. It's not like you could pack your regular wardrobe and toiletries. I had collected a fair share of products from previous dates, but at that moment, I was drawing a blank where half of them were beside my bedroom floor.

"Need help?" Michael asked from the doorway.

I jumped about a foot in the air. Michael was lucky I didn't respond with a ball of electricity to his chest. As it were, my hands were already up in a defensive position, ready to strike.

"You sure you're all right?"

"Yes, sorry. As I said, work's been crazy." I shook my hands to dissipate the energy. "I can't find half of my stuff these days." My room was certainly evidence of that. I was wearing the only clean, appropriately styled dress I owned for our jump back in time. I wondered if I could hire a member of the Agency's Clean-Up Crew to come in here and organize this mess. It wouldn't be nearly as exciting as their regular job—but maybe one of the members would like to make a little side cash.

"It just so happens I thought of that."

"You did?" I cocked my head to the side.

"I stopped by Bloomingdale's. It was for a case," Michael quickly clarified. "But then I saw the dress rack and thought of you."

I visibly paled, which was saying something, seeing as my skin was porcelain to begin with.

"But I can return them." Michael read my expression. "I just thought it would be easier having a wardrobe at the ready given this weekend."

Michael was right. This weekend required plenty of public events, from the rehearsal dinner to the wedding itself and everything in between. If I had my head in the game, I would have outfits laid out for every occasion, like a woman in the early sixties would. "No, you're right. It's smart. So, where are they?"

"At the hotel. I had them shipped there."

"You did?"

"You seem surprised."

"It's just—" I thought before continuing, not wanting to offend Michael. "I guess I'm not used to someone taking care of me." And maybe that was part of my problem with dating Michael. He was a genuinely nice man who cared for me, and I was more used to taking care of myself. I had to be with tracking down the slums of the paranormal world day in and day out.

"I'll try not to make it a habit," Michael winked. "Are you ready, then?"

I took one final look about the room and tossed a couple of necessities into my handbag. "I suppose so. Let's go."

"We're headed out," I said to Agatha as we

descended the staircase. She replied by covering her face with her tan-dipped paw. "Shall I ring you if I need anything?" I added louder than necessary. As my familiar, Agatha was the one person I could get in touch with if things got dicey, and sometimes they did. Agatha buried her face deeper under the paw. "Perhaps you'd like a souvenir from Chicago? A pet goldfish to mesmerize you or some tuna tartare?"

"They don't have tuna tartare in the sixties," Agatha grumbled.

"Just checking to see if you're paying attention."

"Will you knock it off and get getting? Can't you see I'm trying to take a nap here?" Agatha yawned.

"Love you too," I replied in a sing-song voice.

Michael looked at his watch, and I knew he was eager to head out. Generally, I had a specific spell to use for work to jump back in time. All of us cold-case-solving witches used the same one. The spell granted us a week in the past to solve a cold case and included a special clause that our presence in the past wouldn't affect the present. Michael and I used a similar spell in our travels, leaving out the crime's unpunished phrase from the original, but still, rules were rules. We couldn't stay in the other person's time period for more than a week, and we had to make sure not to mess with the future.

With one hand holding my purse and the other

holding Michael's hand, I let him whisk us off into the past.

The past is behind us,
   But close to our hearts.
   Cosmos guide us to depart,
   Time travel to the past,
   No time ripple will last,
   Nineteen sixty-two is our time,
   For an experience that transcends a lifetime.

TWO

The thing about time travel is that some people find it exhilarating, and other people? Well, not so much. I was one of the other people. Don't get me wrong, I loved solving cold cases and kicking criminals' butts, but the actual process of being sucked back in time twisted my tummy and scrambled my head, leaving my world spinning and my skin clammy.

Michael was the former.

"That was something, huh?" A boyish grin sprawled across his face. I, on the other hand, was bracing myself against the mirrored wall of the small space. My purse dangled from the crook in my elbow. I pinched the bridge of my nose with my other hand and tried to steady my breathing and calm my stomach. Michael and I were face-to-face, but knowing how time travel didn't agree with me, he quickly stepped back.

"I'm okay," I said, taking in the space. A floor-length mirror stood before us, and a little bench seat was set off to the side. It was only big enough to hold a purse and maybe a shopping bag or two. Rejected dresses and blouses hung from hooks on the wall. "A fitting room?"

"Pretty clever, right?" Michael replied. And it was. When you traveled back in time, you had to be careful not to pop up in the middle of a busy street or a hotel lobby because that was sure to draw attention. I can use magic to scramble memories, but not an entire pedestrian-filled space. Plus, the fitting room was much more pleasant than the toilet stalls I tended to pop up in.

A knock sounded on the fitting room door. "Is everything okay in there, ma'am?" An older woman's voice came through the door.

"I agree. That dress is lovely. Come on, dear, I'll buy two of them," Michael said, raising his voice and playing the role of the doting husband perfectly.

"Are you sure? They are quite expensive," I replied, playing along.

"Nothing is too expensive for my girl."

"Excuse me, sir." A series of rapid knocks rapped

the door. "These are women-only fitting rooms! Sir?" The attendant's voice was one notch below shrill.

Michael grabbed an armful of discarded garments and swung open the door. "We'll take these. Bag them up, will you?" Michael thrust the clothes at the woman, who quickly bit her tongue as she scrambled to contain the fabric that overfilled her arms and mentally calculated her commission.

"What do you say? On to handbags, my dear?" Michael said to me over his shoulder.

"Lead the way, honey."

And Michael did, taking me by the hand and walking us right past the handbags, down the elevator, and out the front door.

As we stepped outside, I took a deep breath of fresh air and felt the last lingering wisps of time travel dissipate from me. It was a warm, late spring day. The sunshine felt good on my face, and the soft breeze swept my bangs back from my forehead. For years I'd rocked a pixie cut, sometimes spikes and all, but over the last couple of months, I had let the cut grow out, softening my look ever so slightly. The style made it easier to blend in without requiring a magical makeover every time I blasted off to the past.

Clear-headed at last, I was immediately struck by how open everything was.

"Are you sure this is the Magnificent Mile?" I'd

visited the high-end shopping district, with its upscale shops, trendy eateries, and posh hotels, a dozen times. It was one of the reasons I was eager to return to Chicago. Everyone has their favorite big city, and the Windy City was mine. But there was still no Sears Tower insight—well, Willis Tower, I guess it's called now. No Hancock building either. Heck, I didn't even see a Tiffany & Co. or a Bloomingdale's. Instead, I spotted shops like Blum's Vogue and Bonwit Teller, a little boutique called Bes-Ben Shop with the most elaborate and whimsical hats I'd ever seen. I was going to have to stop in there.

However, there was one store on the corner of Michigan Avenue and East Chicago Avenue that lasted through the decades, and that was Walgreens. Kitty-corner from that was the beautiful, gothic-styled Chicago Water Tower. The tower looked more like a church than a municipal city building with its distinctive yellow Joliet limestone exterior and castellated accents climbing twelve stories. It dominated the landscape. The architectural beauty no longer pumped water, but it was still lovely to admire both in nineteen sixty-two and today.

Don't get me wrong, it was busy here, but it wasn't like modern-day Chicago. The majority of the buildings were more low rise than high rise, and the billboards were something else. The giant neon

Coca-Cola sign with a digital clock below it was my favorite. On the opposite building, and just as impressive, was a billboard advertising Pall Mall cigarettes. The brand promised a satisfying flavor that would be friendly to your tastes and featured a giant pineapple with a pack of cigarettes propped up against it. Even so, the skyline wasn't as jam-packed and congested as the Chicago of today, and somehow, that made it better. I would have never believed it possible before, but the sixties had grown on me. I did a quick circle to take it all in. With its fitted bodice and full skirt, my belted swing dress ballooned out about me.

"It's different, but I like it," I said to myself as much to Michael. "So, what's the game plan?"

"We're staying at The Duke Hotel up here, along with the rest of the wedding guests. I thought we could get settled and grab an early lunch, and then Jim, that's the groom, wants the guys to go and pick up our tuxes. After that, he said something about shooting at the club."

"Clay shooting?" I had never been, but it always looked fun. Something about yelling, "Pull!" with a shotgun at the ready seemed like a smashing good time.

"I wish. I'd take a gun any day over a bow, but Jim's into archery. So off to the country club we go."

"Which is where the wedding is taking place?"

"Correct. But Mr. Rigatti, that's the bride's father, insisted that all of the wedding guests stay in luxury. Hence why we're all at The Duke."

"Got it."

Michael stopped walking, and I did the same. "I think this afternoon is a guys-only thing, but the bride, Mary, has activities planned for the ladies if you want to join them."

I pictured a group of women at the salon getting their nails done and hair set. I scrunched my nose.

Michael chuckled. "That's what I thought, but I wanted to leave it up to you." We started walking again.

"Listen, don't worry about me this weekend. You do what you have to do. I'm fine on my own and would love to explore this rendition of Chicago." A mint green boat of a car drove down Michigan Avenue, followed by a similar-sized car, this time buttercup yellow. You didn't see cars these colors every day anymore. It seemed like modern-day car trends were all about neutral tones such as white, black, gray, and silver. In other words, boring. I couldn't wait to see what other treasures the city held.

We arrived at The Duke after a ten-minute walk. The hotel appeared to be about fifteen stories high and dominated several smaller neighboring outlets. The white brick building sported a black awning and was tall and narrow like a rectangular block stood on its end. The hotel's street address was stamped on the front in gold lettering, and a green carpet was rolled out front. The doorman, wearing a gray, pressed suit with brass buttons, opened the door for us to enter. I replied with a thank you, but my pace faltered when my foot crossed the threshold. The overwhelming power of magic hit me in the face. Shocked, I turned back and looked at Michael for an explanation.

"The hotel is a favorite for our kind," he replied, his voice barely above a whisper. Placing his hand on the small of my back, he led me forward toward the check-in counter.

By our kind, I assumed he meant all supernaturals because there were more than a couple witches here in residence. Quite a bit more if my nose was any indication. The air was thick with the woodsy scent of shifters, and I found myself mentally calculating if we were anywhere near the full moon.

I took in my surroundings while Michael checked us in. The Duke reminded me of glamour from a bygone era. The owners had decorated the lobby in an Italian renaissance style with crystal chandeliers dangling from coffered ceilings, navy tufted chairs dotted the elegant public spaces, and potted ferns added just the right amount of greenery. Even the red patterned carpet with its blue and gold inlays felt plush beneath my feet. If only my magical antenna could turn down a notch, I might be able to relax a bit.

I joined the conversation when Michael inquired after our luggage.

"Yes, Mr. Cooper. Your bags arrived this morning." The front desk man snapped his fingers, and a bellhop jumped to attention. "Please take Mr. Cooper and his guest, Miss—" the gentleman left it open for Michael to fill in.

"Harper," I answered for him.

"Please take Mr. Cooper and Ms. Harper to room 401."

"Yes, sir. Right this way, please," the bellhop said to us. Before we could even make it to the elevator, a trail of bellhops joined after us with carts in tow. I did a double-take over my shoulder at the number of dresses hanging from the carts and hat boxes stacked beneath them.

"I thought they'd all look good on you," Michael said by way of explanation.

I had to shut my mouth so I would quit gaping at Michael's purchases.

"Would it make you feel better if I told you they

were on sale?" Michael said as we stepped into the elevator.

"A little bit." I recalled the rows and rows of discounted dresses, coats, and slacks at my first visit to New York City's department stores of yesteryear. It was impossible to beat the pricing. You could snag a meticulously tailored dress for twenty dollars or less. Pants and sweaters were around five dollars, and that was full price. Michael lived in a sparsely furnished one-bedroom shoebox in downtown Manhattan and claimed he didn't need much. Like me, he was the job and only slept at his apartment, but still, I knew those dresses hadn't come cheap, sale or not. Maybe I should pay him back. I eyed Michael as we rode the elevator up. He responded by reaching for my hand and squeezing it. I decided to drop it for now.

* * *

Michael and I didn't stay at the hotel for long, sticking to our plan and heading out for lunch. Michael left it to me to pick. Being a vegetarian in the past isn't as tricky as it might initially seem. The food in this period was less processed, particularly at restaurants where you could talk to the chef directly. We ended up choosing to dine at Jacques French Restaurant in the 900 Building. The restaurant stood on the corner of Delaware and Michigan, and I knew it was where Bloomingdale's stood today. It was impossible not to adore the restaurant, with its outdoor gardens and seating that would've recently opened for the season. The green and orange striped umbrellas stood like domes over the small bistro tables. A small fountain in the center of the court-yard was the space's focal point. I ordered an omelet with asparagus tips for fifty cents and added a side of potatoes mashed in cream for thirty-five cents. Michael was the big spender with his whole cold lobster served with homemade mayonnaise for two dollars and twenty-five cents. When the waiter offered us each a glass of the house champagne for seventy-five cents, I was going to turn it down until I reminded myself that I was, after all, on vacation and, for once, not on a case. Plus, when was the last time I'd sipped champagne in the sunshine with my boyfriend? I'll tell you when, never.

After lunch, Michael and I parted ways, and I stopped in at Bonwit Teller, which turned out to be a luxury department store. The high-end store combined art with fashion. Avant-garde window displays by the likes of Salvador Dali highlighted the trends of Italian-born designer Elsa Schiaparelli and the French fashion house Lanvin. With its Art Deco fabric hanging in the fitting rooms, decorative murals, and perfume wafting in the air, shopping at Bonwit

Teller was an out-of-this-world experience, leaving me feeling pampered. The day was full of firsts.

After that, I stopped by that marvelous hat shop I had spotted earlier. The hats weren't practical, and they were pricey even by twenty-first-century standards, but I loved them nonetheless. If I could justify a time and place to wear a red-felted hat with little pony figurines stacked about, I would've snatched it up, or even scooped it up as a souvenir if the price was a bit cheaper. Something about those Bes-Ben hats made me smile. I left the hat shop and was called next door to the bakery by the delectable window display, which included baskets of lemon twists, rainbow cookies, and Italian horns, and those were the ones I knew. If that's what the window display showcased, I couldn't wait to see what else was in store. It was official: I was a rebel. First, breaking my relationship rules, then glasses of champagne at lunch, and now dessert. Lexi would be proud of me.

I opened the quaint Italian bakery's door. The sweet aroma of powdered sugar and chocolate greeted me. My mouth got tingly thinking about the sugar rush that was to come. An impressive glass display case ran the length of the bakery and contained everything from breads and rolls on one end to sweeter offerings like cream cakes and puffed pastries on the other. A dozen or so tables made up the rest of the rectangular space. The soft yellow walls had welcoming phrases in Italian hand-painted here and there. At least that's what I think they were.

"Buon giorno, what can I get for you?" the older woman asked in a thick Italian accent behind the counter. The baker had dark gray hair tucked under a black headscarf and olive-toned skin. She wasn't quite five feet tall.

"You have a lovely bakery. I'm having a hard time choosing," I confessed, staring at the expansive case.

"Crostata then. You'll have de crostata," she replied with a nod and confidently walked away before I could answer.

"Okay," I agreed, not knowing what a crostata was.

Within a minute, I had a thick slice of a berry tart in my possession, along with a frothy cappuccino.

"Itza blackberry," the woman said in her lovely accent as she handed the crostata over. I thanked her and went to take a seat at a nearby table. I could get used to this vacation thing. I dug my fork into the sweet dessert that reminded me of pie.

A young woman hurried into the bakery moments later while I savored my treat. Two other ladies came in and joined her. I'd guess they were in their early twenties, but they appeared wildly different in their mannerisms. A brunette with a sleek, low ponytail stood to one side. She talked a mile a minute, seemingly egging her on. "It's your wedding. You should have what you want!" I heard her say as she marched her distraught friend to the front counter. Tears were in the young woman's eyes. Her expression was apprehensive as her hand unconsciously fidgeted with her pearl necklace. The woman's countenance seemed out of place for such a cheery place. The other friend lagged behind, swaying her skirt absentmindedly and looking about the bakery without a care in the world.

Patrons continued to nibble on the pastries and sip their coffees. I attempted to do the same.

"Miss Rigatti, what do you need?" the baker asked.

I snapped my head up at the mention of the last name. Wasn't that the bride's last name from this weekend?

"Well, I don't know. It's foolish, Mrs. Lucci." The young woman twisted her necklace around her finger rather nervously.

Mrs. Lucci eyed the bride suspiciously and waited for her to continue. When she didn't, the fast-talking brunette flatly stated, "Mary hates vanilla cake." The name Mary confirmed it. She was the bride of this weekend's wedding.

"Che cos'è questo? What's this? But that is what you ordered," Mrs. Lucci replied.

"I know! I don't know what I was thinking. Actually, I do. Papa loves white cake. A big white cake is what he wants for me. But I don't like it. Not one bit," Mary replied, her curled, chin-length blonde hair swaying as she shook her head, threatening to tip the pink pillbox hat that balanced precariously on top of her head. "And now I don't know what to do. I don't want to disappoint Papa. He's done so much for me. What if it makes him angry? I hate conflict."

"As much as you hate vanilla cake?" the fast-talking friend interjected.

Mary seemed to weigh the options.

"I love vanilla cake," the lollygagging friend chimed in.

"That's great, Ruthie. When you get married, you can eat all the vanilla cake you want. But this isn't about you right now," the brunette snapped.

"Cosa ti aspetti che faccia? What do you expect me to do? Mi dispiace, but the cake is baked." Mrs. Lucci continued to question the bride in a mixture of Italian and English, agitation growing in her voice and her arms flapping about as the brunette joined in, yelling at the baker. That was a mistake. For a petite older woman, Mrs. Lucci could argue with the best of them.

"Mama, what is the matter?" A younger woman came out from the back kitchen to interrupt the quarrel. Her bright orange scarf held back a mass of dark curls, and flour powdered her dark blue apron. Mrs. Lucci replied to her daughter in Italian. The woman's arms punctuated her sentences as she talked with her hands, and her eyes glared at the trio.

"It was ridiculous of me to think I could change it. I'm such an idiot!" Mary buried her face in her hands, her hat surprisingly staying in place as the tears fell.

"Who's an idiot?" Ruthie asked in a slow, dreamy voice.

"Wait, you're telling me there's nothing you can do?" The brunette looked around the bakery in disbelief. "All these cakes, and you can't fix this?"

"Mi arrendo! What would you like me to do? Bake a new cake? Itza wedding cake, not tiramisu. Should've baked a millefoglie! Sponge cake, bah!" Mrs. Lucci blustered and then turned to her daughter, "Don't look at me like that, Rosa. You know there isn't time."

Rosa admonished her mother in their native tongue, yet she still didn't offer a solution.

Thankfully, I thought of one.

I stood up and walked over to the group of women. "Excuse me, hi. My name's Vee. I'm a guest at your wedding this weekend. My boyfriend, Michael, is your best man." The ladies all stared at me as if wondering where I had come from. I quickly continued, "I couldn't help overhearing your story. I have an idea." The group looked at me expectantly. "What if you create a smaller cake on the side, and the bride and groom can share a piece from that one? That way, you don't have to change anything about the wedding cake."

The ladies blinked at me, and no one spoke for a beat until the bride said, "Is that possible? Could you do something like that?" Mary looked hopefully to Mrs. Lucci, who, for her part, threw her hands up in exasperation and walked away.

It was the daughter, Rosa, who replied. "Si. We could do that," she said confidently. "What flavor are you thinking?"

I left the group to finalize the cake and sat down to finish my pastry and coffee, but if I was expecting that to be the end of the wedding cake drama, I was sorely mistaken.

A few minutes later, Rosa offered Mary and her friends cake samples to choose from.

"I'm too nervous to eat," Mary fanned herself and looked away from the cake.

"Well, I'm not," the brunette replied. She seemed like the most outgoing one in the group. Without waiting for a reply, she stabbed a forkful of chocolate cake and put it in her mouth. "Mmm, yep. Joe will like that one." She swallowed it down and eyed another bite.

"It's Jim," Mary replied.

The friend didn't reply. The second bite of cake was still on her fork, and the words were barely out of her mouth before the young women's body went limp and she hit the floor.

"Barbara Jean!" Mary hollered, bending down to help her friend, but it was lights out. The woman wasn't moving a muscle, and her eyes were wide open.

"Wow, I can't believe she fell over like that," Ruthie said to no one in particular.

"Help! Someone call an ambulance," Mary said frantically from the ground while cradling Barbara Jean's head in her lap. I stood to look for a phone, but Rosa was already on it.

* * *

The paramedics arrived within five minutes. Bakery patrons left bits of cannoli and cups of coffee on the tables as they filed outside to give the medics room to work.

"She has a pulse," I said to the medics as they took over, and that's all I could say. Mary had tried to get Barbara Jean to snap out of it by talking to her, but I wasn't sure what else to do short of slapping her. She hadn't choked but rather passed out stone-cold. Barbara Jean looked like a statue, frozen in place.

A couple of uniformed officers arrived on the scene seconds after the medics.

"Another one? You've got to be kidding me. Randle's going to lose it," one cop said to the other.

I looked to Mary and Rosa, but neither seemed to know who the officers were talking about.

"Better call it in," the second officer said.

"Nuh-uh. You do it. Randle bit my head off the last time," the first officer replied.

"Play you for it," the second one said.

The officers wordlessly began playing a round of rock, paper, scissors, neither one of them seeming too concerned about helping Barbara Jean.

The first officer won, leaving the second officer to call Randle. "Fine, but next time, you're calling him, even if you do win." He huffed and headed back outside.

We backed up and allowed the paramedics to attend to Barbara Jean. Mary stood beside me, her hand clutched around her pearl necklace. A blotchy rash rose and spread across her fair complexion.

"What in the world happened to poor Barbara Jean?" Mary said to me. "I should call her mama, but I can't even think straight."

"Do you have the number? I can make the call for you," I offered. Mary didn't, but she gave me the woman's full name, and it was actually Rosa who made the call, using the operator to connect the line.

Then I thought about Michael. He was a healer. Unlike some witches, it wasn't a talent that Michael came by naturally, but rather something his sister insisted he studied once becoming a cop.

"Do you want me to try and get a hold of Michael? He might be able to help."

"Your boyfriend's a doctor?" Ruthie asked.

"Not exactly." I looked at Mary knowingly, waiting for her to catch on.

Realization crossed her face. "Thanks, but I don't think he'll be able to help *her*." The emphasis of the last word came across to me meaning her kind. Barbara Jean was a supernatural of some sort and not a witch.I nodded in understanding and said a prayer that the regular doctors would be able to work their own magic.

* * *

The paramedics exited the bakery with Barbara Jean on the stretcher. Mary was still in shock.

"Maybe she had a heart attack?" the dreamy friend said. "Or a sugar rush? You know how foggy your head gets when you eat too much sugar?" The friend looked at me to back her up, but I was at a loss for words.

"Sometimes I wonder about you, Ruthie," Mary replied.

"What did I miss?" A feisty redhead rushed through the bakery doors and surveyed the scene.

"Nancy, what in the heavens are you doing here? You're not still chasing ambulances, are you?" Mary asked the young woman.

Nancy waved Mary's question away. "Give me the scoop," she replied, paper and pen at the ready. A 35mm camera swayed from the strap around her neck.

"I'll do no such thing. It's Barbara Jean in that ambulance. Have some respect," Mary shot back, disdain heavy in her voice. Mary turned away to look out the bakery's front window.

Nancy took that as her opening. "Is she dead?" she whispered to me.

I shook my head. The expression was more of, "I can't believe you're asking me that," rather than a yes or a no.

"Hope I got a decent picture of the ambulance," Nancy said to herself before turning to me. "Depending on what went down here, I might have a cover story."

Ruthie nodded empathetically before Mary

interjected. "Nancy! I can't believe you. I swear." The rash had spread down Mary's face, making her chest and hands blotchy.

"Geesh, I'm only trying to do my job," Nancy replied but walked away.

"I tell you what, if she weren't Jim's friend, I wouldn't have booked her for the wedding," Mary folded her arms and watched Nancy sidle up to Rosa and Mrs. Lucci.

"She's your wedding photographer?" I asked.

Mary rolled her eyes. "Don't even get me started."

I left the comment at that because, at that moment, a man I presumed to be Detective Randle walked into the bakery. He was a block of a man with a square head, broad shoulders, and thick legs. He appeared to have given up on shaving and ironing his shirts. He walked up to us and yanked the toothpick out of his mouth. Nothing was left but splinters on one end, which he now seemed to be chewing.

"Which one of you can tell me what went on here?" the detective asked while scanning the bakery and not meeting our eyes.

I looked over to Mary with her head-to-toe rash and tears in her eyes and figured it would be best if I took the lead. Who knows what Ruthie would say. That poor girl had her head in the clouds.

I cleared my throat. "I can tell you what

happened." I gave a rundown of what happened to Barbara Jean, starting from the moment the women walked through the bakery doors. The whole recap took less than two minutes.

"And who are you exactly?" Detective Randle asked.

"A friend of a friend," I replied.

"Who just happened to witness everything?" The detective met my gaze for the first time. I stared right back, with nothing to hide.

Detective Randle shuffled his feet over to the bakery counter, where the remaining cake samples sat untouched. "This the cake?"

We all nodded. "Si," Mrs. Lucci replied.

"You bake this?" Detective Randle asked Mrs. Lucci directly.

"Si," she replied more defiantly, daring the detective to criticize her baking.

The detective sniffed it, wrinkled his nose, and put it down. "Did your friend have any health problems?" he asked no one in particular.

It was Mary that spoke up. "I don't think so. She seemed perfectly fine today until she—" Mary's emotions got the best of her, and she couldn't finish her sentence.

"I think she had a sugar rush," Ruthie told the detective, who in turn eyed Ruthie like she might have a screw loose. "Have you ever had one of those?" Ruthie blinked up innocently.

"I'm getting too old for this," the detective said to himself. He folded his arms and nodded his head for a moment before shrugging his shoulders and walking out as if lost in thought.

"Is that it?" Mary asked.

"Good question," I replied. The detective hadn't taken down our contact information or even collected a sample of the cake, which I was sure he should have. I didn't want Mrs. Lucci coming after me, but what if Barbara Jean had been poisoned? Wouldn't the detective want to rule that out?

The detective might be done with us, but I wasn't done with him.

THREE

I said goodbye to Mary and stepped outside to find the detective. I didn't find him, but I did find Nancy waiting for me.

"Hey, wait up," she said. I begrudgingly obeyed. "My name is Nancy Bolton, and you're a witch, I know it," Nancy proclaimed.

"Excuse me?"

"Sorry, I shouldn't have blurted it out like that. People tell me I'm too direct. But I can't help it. It's a handy trait for a reporter to have. I'm a witch too, which is how I know you are. I can sense magic. I always thought it was a lame gift, but not now. You're looking at the editor of the Midnight Express," Nancy proudly declared. "It's a supernatural newspaper. I created it. Have you ever been to New York City?"

I nodded.

"Have you read their supernatural newsies?"

"Yes." Michael introduced me to them during my first case in NYC. The supernatural papers in New York City were a treasure trove of information for the magical community. They covered everything from politics in the form of shifter pack elections to community events such as the Annual Witches Cauldron Benefit. And if you needed a new broom or a vampire for hire, the classifieds had you covered. This was in addition to the local and regional news you'd expect a newspaper to feature. In the pre-internet period, newspapers were vital to keeping the community informed, including supernaturals.

"So, you know all about them. Mind if I ask you a couple of questions? I'm trying to get to the bottom of all of this."

"You and me both," I mumbled. Where did the detective run off to? Given the officers' comments, Barbara Jean wasn't the first person to pass out under suspicious circumstances.

Nancy looked at me with raised eyebrows.

"Sorry, you wanted to ask me something?"

"Right. Did Barbara Jean look scared or anything beforehand?"

"Scared? No, I don't think so."

"Shoot, there goes that theory."

"What theory?"

"I was hoping that maybe a spook was going around scaring people to death. It made sense with the other three victims. I've been calling them the 'Scared to Death' cases. But, as far as I know, this is the first time there have been witnesses."

"What can you tell me about the other cases?"

"You haven't heard about them?"

"I'm from out of town," I explained.

"Well, the first victim was an heiress, who also happened to be a witch. Her best friend found her in the foyer, sprawled out, eyes wide open, but she was too far gone for anyone to help her."

"That's horrible. And there wasn't any sign of forced entry or injury?"

"Nope. It looked like she just dropped dead, which you know, happens from time to time. It probably wouldn't have made the news if it wasn't for her fortune. Mrs. Stein's husband made his money in oil and left his wife every penny. Honestly, that's the only reason I picked the piece up and ran it. A rich witch suddenly keeling over was enough to make the front page. I thought that would be the end of it until two days later when another victim turned up."

"Who was it this time?"

"An old shifter, Bernie Compton. He was a pack

organizer back in his day but retired out of politics decades ago."

"Tell me more about what he did exactly." I knew little of shifter politics but wondered if maybe there was a clue there.

"Well, you know a shifter pack is like a supernatural gang, but bigger. Maybe a union is a better analogy. Anyway, you want the strong shifters on your side. Bernie did that. He recruited shifters to support his pack. But that was years ago. As far as I can tell, he's kept his paws out of politics the last decade, at least."

"And he was found just like Mrs. Stein?"

"More or less. He was at his apartment doing laundry in the basement when he fell over and died. At least that's what's been assumed. I interviewed his wife, and she told me that she went to check on him after he had been gone for a couple of hours. She found him on the cement floor, eyes wide open but no pulse, just like Mrs. Stein."

"And that's when you started to think something supernatural might be afoot?"

"I started to think it was a real possibility. Reporters don't often believe in coincidences."

I wanted to tell Nancy that neither did detectives.

"Then the third case popped up yesterday."

Wow, Nacy was just full of information.

"Another shifter?" I guessed.

"No. A vampire hunter named Xavier James." The young witch's eye lit up, retelling the tale.

"Really?" If you thought time-traveling witches were rare, vampire hunters were even more so. They looked like regular humans, but often there was vampire blood somewhere in the family tree. Vampire hunters tended not to mess with us regular supernatural folks, and instead went after the rogue vampires who insisted on murdering people. It was well-known that vampires didn't need to drain and kill humans to survive. Often all it took was a little bit of supernatural glamour, and a donor would wake up a couple of hours later none the wiser. And yet some vampires insisted on being the monsters of nightmares. They were the ones vampire hunters targeted.

Nancy nodded. "He was found unresponsive in his truck over at the community center. It looked like he had finished a workout and was heading home when he passed out. Luckily for him, another community center member found him, called the paramedics, and got him help."

"Where is he now?" Not that I was going to interview him, I tried to tell myself.

"This minute? I don't know. Probably still in the hospital, but he wouldn't talk to me. The paramedics did, though. They said he looked frozen in fear. So, I thought a ghost was wreaking havoc on our community." Nancy shrugged.

"And these victims, what do they have in common?" I couldn't help looking for a motive.

"Nothing that I've been able to turn up. I mean, besides the supernatural community."

"There has to be something."

"Trust me. I know that. I just don't know what it is."

Details of the cases stuck with me as I made my way back to The Duke. Michael was still out, which gave me plenty of time to pace the hotel room and think. A couple of days was hardly enough time to solve a case. Heck, half the time, a week was not enough time, and that's when I was officially assigned one. Then again, this wasn't a cold case. For all I knew, Detective Randle or even Nancy would solve the mystery any day now. True, I wasn't very confident in Detective Randle because, as far as I could tell, he wasn't a supernatural, and this case had magic dripping all over it. But Nancy was, and she seemed to be pretty decent with her interview skills based on the information she shared with me. But it still bothered me. I needed to know if these cases were ever solved.

The more I paced, the more I knew what I

needed to do. Only I wasn't sure if I had enough magic at the ready. I had never attempted a time jump and astral projection on the same day. When you used astral projection, your physical body remained unconscious in one spot while you projected yourself to another. The fact that I had to pick another place to project to and another time made it all the more challenging.

That's where Agatha came into play. As my familiar, she was the easiest for me to connect to. The last thing I wanted was for my astral body to be stuck aimlessly out in the ether. I shuddered at the prospect.

I took a second to get comfortable on the bed and relax, letting my magic slowly release inside. Slowly, bright colors started to appear in my peripheral vision. Bursts of oranges, reds, and pinks flashed and popped like silent fireworks. Soft piano music began to play in my head, lulling me to relax and let go. I felt myself pull free, lifting off into the great unknown. Below me, everything felt heavy, but the higher I flew, the lighter and more colorful everything became. The bursts of light turned into streaks until the entire landscape was filled with swaths of color. I was floating high and feeling free, but perhaps a bit too free. In the distance, I could see Agatha. She was still snoozing on the back of the couch, her paws on top of her ears. The scene was hazy, and I couldn't bring it into focus or get any closer. I felt like no matter how long I floated there, I couldn't reach her. I didn't have the power to break through the other side.

"Agatha!" I called out, my voice echoing in my ears. "Wake up!"

I tried to push forward but no luck. I was floating aimlessly, with no means to move forward or go back, and the longer I stayed adrift, the harder it would be to get home.

Don't panic, I told myself, even though I felt the anxiety building in my chest. My heart hammered, and I had nothing to hold on to, nothing to bring me to my senses. I had two choices: succumb to the fear, or find the courage within me to pull myself together.

It wasn't easy.

It took all my power to bring my thoughts under control. I focused every ounce of energy I had left and called out to Agatha again, this time in my mind. My plea was simple.

"Agatha, help."

Agatha's eyes darted open. Her head snapped to attention, and she jumped off the couch, searching for me. I hadn't seen my feline familiar dart around the house that fast in ages, not even when she chased a country mouse.

"In here," I said, meaning her head.

Hearing my voice again, Agatha nodded. I watched as she sat motionlessly and closed her eyes. It felt like forever, but in reality, it was probably only a minute before Agatha joined me on the astral plane. She was no longer an old snarky cat but a beautiful young witch with long, jet-black hair and sparkling emerald eyes. She floated to me effortlessly.

"What's going on?" she asked.

"I may have stumbled onto a case. Four members of the supernatural community, all mysteriously attacked in Chicago the summer of nineteen sixty-two. Look into it for me?"

"Sure thing. I'll reach out to the Bureau. Anything else?" Agatha went to lick her wrist. Old habits die hard.

"Help me back?"

Agatha gave a Cheshire Cat-like grin and gave my shoulders a shove. It was all I needed. I somer-saulted backward like an unwilling passenger on the salt and pepper shaker ride at the carnival. I landed with an OOMPH back in my body. Coughing, I sat up and sucked in air, trying to catch my breath.

Ugh, never again, I thought, no astral projecting and time jumping on the same day. That had been a mistake.

I closed my eyes. My head was still whirling

when a knock came at the door. For a moment, I thought I may have imagined it until I heard it again. Opening my eyes, it took me a second to regain my focus.

"Coming," I called, so the visitor knew I had heard them. I was unsteady on my feet as I made my way across the room. It felt like I was walking sideways, heavily leaning to my left. Steadying against the door, I peered out the peephole and saw that it was one of the bellhops from check-in. The young man folded his hands behind his back, and he had a smile on his face.

"Yes?" I said as I opened the door and greeted him.

"This just came by special post for you, ma'am." The bellhop unclasped his hands and held out a white $8\frac{1}{2}$" x 11" envelope.

My eyebrows shot up in surprise. That was fast, I thought, recognizing the case file from the Agency of Paranormal Peculiarities. I thanked the young man and opened the envelope before the door shut. I took the folder over to the bed and sat down on edge to read through its contents.

The file mirrored what Nancy had already told me. It seemed that when the string of strange cases stopped and the trail turned cold, the city police department dropped the investigation. Without any suspects or motives, I was forced to start with the victims at ground zero. That was okay. I was used to it. Inside the envelope were a few newspaper clippings, which I was about to pull out, but stopped short. I heard the key in the lock seconds before Michael opened the door, but it was enough time for me to toss the case file under the bed. The last thing I wanted to do was distract Michael from his friends and the wedding. He deserved some downtime and not worrying about a case for once. Not that I would keep everything from him. I was going to tell him about Barbara Jean, but that was the extent of it. The same went for the rest of the bridal party, especially Mary. What bride wanted a homicidal supernatural being running around town on her wedding weekend?

I hopped off the bed, perhaps a bit eagerly, and met Michael with a welcoming kiss. At least I didn't shock him this time.

"How was shooting?" I asked.

If Michael was suspicious, he didn't say anything. "Good. I learned I'm not much of an archer, but we had fun. How was your afternoon around the city?"

"It was nice. I checked out that hat shop I told you about, and I even found an authentic Italian bakery." I couldn't help the grimace that followed.

"Your facial expression has me dying to try them out," Michael replied dryly.

"Ha, ha. No, the baked goods were fine. It was the bride who wasn't."

"Not Mary."

"Yes, Mary."

"Tell me she's not as awful as I fear."

"What? No. She's a bit nervous, but she seemed okay. You haven't met her?"

"Afraid not. I didn't even know Jim had a girl, and then BAM! He's asking me to be his best man. It's all gone down real fast."

"Ah, well, she seemed lovely actually, but her bridesmaid passed out right there during the cake tasting. Stone cold. They had to call an ambulance and everything. Mary was pretty shaken up."

"She okay?"

"I honestly don't know. I'm sure we'll find out more tonight."

"I'm sure we will."

FOUR

Tonight was the first official wedding event – a meet and greet with the entire wedding party and their significant others. We were to meet in the hotel lobby at seven o'clock and, as a group, walk down to the Bowl-O-Rama, a neighborhood bowling alley, for a few games of bowling and pizza, which is why, after spending a couple of relaxing hours with Michael, I found myself getting ready for a night on the town. Honestly, the way fashion circled back around, my outfit tonight wasn't that different from what I would wear for an evening out in the twenty-first century. I slipped on a pair of ankle-length, high-waisted black leggings and paired it with a gray sleeveless mock neck sweater, adding a burgundy and white patterned headscarf as a neckerchief. I kept my footwear simple with black ballet flats.

"If I didn't know any better, I'd swear you were born and raised in the sixties.

Michael's comment got a smile out of me.

"Why, thank you. I try." When it came to fashion, men had it so much easier. No matter the decade, it seemed all they had to do was tug on a pair of dress pants and a button-up shirt, and they were good to go —a theory I was all the more convinced of since dating Michael. He rarely had to alter his wardrobe no matter what decade we went out to dinner unless he wanted to follow a trend or hit the gym with me.

Mary and Jim stood next to an oversized, polished mahogany table in the center of the lobby. Jim stood behind his bride-to-be with his hands on her shoulders. Another couple that I hadn't met yet stood on the other side of them, the man talking to Jim. Ruthie, the space cadet, and her rather eccentric date stood off to the side, waiting for the rest of us to arrive.

"Is everyone a supe?" I asked Michael out of the corner of my mouth, eyeing Ruthie's date. He was dressed head to toe in black. He wore his dark hair greased back. An elongated nose set off his triangular face. He stood there, snapping his fingers and bee bopping even though a soft piano concerto floated from the lobby's overhead speakers.

"I think so," Michael replied, scanning the group.

"Michael, glad you could join us," Jim said, taking his hand from Mary's shoulder and extending it to shake Michael's.

"Absolutely. This is my girlfriend, Vee. Vee, this is Jim and Mary."

I shook Jim's hand and then Mary's, adding a soft smile. "We met earlier," I said to the group.

"I'm Frank, and this is my wife, Dotty," the man next to Jim said, thrusting out his hand for me to shake. Once I did, he pumped my hand up and down enthusiastically like a used car salesman.

"We're the Pearsons," Dotty added with a strained smile. Either Dotty always wore white silk gloves and fancy dresses to the bowling alley, or she'd never stepped foot in one. At this point, I thought either scenario was possible.

"Carl coming?" Michael asked the guys.

Jim shook his head and left it at that, but Frank didn't.

"Ha! Boy's drunk as a skunk. We left him to sleep it off," Frank replied like it was hilarious. His wife turned up her nose in disgust. "Can't hold his liquor like a Southern boy can!" Frank continued, his laughter booming in the cavernous space.

"How's Barbara Jean?" I asked Mary while Frank continued his obnoxious rhetoric.

"It's too early to tell. Her mama said she came to,

but only for a minute." Mary wiped the tears that started to swell in the corner of her eyes.

"I'm sorry. Forget I asked." I rubbed Mary's shoulder, making a mental note not to ask about the waylaid bridesmaid anymore.

"Shall we then?" Jim asked the group.

I looked over to Ruthie's date. He was walking around, sniffing the air. His nose wrinkled, and nostrils flared as he followed the hunt of an unknown-to-me scent.

Michael took me by the hand. "Hm?" I said in response.

"You ready to go?" Michael asked me quietly.

An amused smile filled my features as Ruthie's date inhaled deeply through his nose as if he was smelling a rose or a delicious meal. Ruthie gazed at him with adoration. Tonight ought to be interesting.

* * *

"Why are we walking? How much further is it? I told you we should've taken a cab, Frank. Oh wait, there's one now. Grab it, Frank! Frank, are you listening to me?" Dotty's voice grew in agitation with every click her high heels made down the sidewalk. I hoped she wouldn't act that way the whole night. You know how it went. It took only one bad apple to wreck a pie. It was the same with nights out. One person complaining was all it took to ruin it. No one liked a party pooper. I tried to tune Dotty out and instead take in the city sights—the flashing lights, neon signs, classic cars, and other city-goers out for a good time. It was a Mecca for the senses. But Dotty was hard to ignore. She turned her shoulders inward whenever another person passed us and sneered at every smile. Heaven forbid someone would accidentally bump into her.

We were only fifteen minutes into the walk when I heard her say something about calling her mother. Frank ignored her. He was too busy talking Jim's ear off. Unfortunately, Jim wasn't even listening. He held Mary's hand and checked to make sure she was okay with walking the rest of the way. Ruthie and her date fell behind the group, and they were in no hurry to speed up their snail's pace, her date darting his attention in response to every sound and smell.

We were at the bowling alley, well into the second game before the two of them turned up. Dotty had downright refused to bowl once she saw the shoes, and she wouldn't drink either. "What do you mean they don't have Booth's?" she said to Frank when he informed her she'd have to drink the house gin in her martini. "And no lemon? You know I always take my martini with a twist of lemon. Who can stand olives?"

At that point, I was more than happy to tip back a bottle of Schlitz, as was Mary, and darn it if I wasn't determined to make sure the bride-to-be had a good time. I could tell Barbara Jean was on her mind, and who could blame her? But I still wanted Mary to have fun. You only got married once, so they say. In a worst-case scenario, I could use my magic to alter Mary's memory and take some of the worries away, but that would only be as a last resort.

When it was my turn, I enthusiastically rolled the eight-pound black resin ball toward the pins. It weaved this way and that way down the oiled surface before landing in the metal gutter with a thud.

"It's okay. You'll get it next time!" Jim hollered from the pit. It was the same thing he said the last three and a half innings.

"I want a new partner," Michael teased from the galley.

I scrunched my face in his direction. So, I couldn't bowl worth a darn. Good thing I was skilled in other areas. When the ball came back from the return, I was ready to hit some pins—my way. I made my approach, releasing the ball smoothly from my hand. Like before, my attempt looked hopeless as the ball teetered dangerously close to the gutter, but magically, at the last possible second, the ball straightened and smashed all the pins down in a rather impressive display of power.

"Strike!" I threw my arms up in success, and the light brightened overhead in a power surge.

"Hot diggity!" Mary exclaimed, jumping up and clapping.

"That's the way!" Jim added.

Michael shook his head and laughed.

"Too much?" I whispered to Michael as I joined his side.

"Nah," Michael replied with a smile and a kiss on the top of my head.

"Couldn't have you switching partners on me now, could I?" I replied.

"Gutter balls and all, there's no one else I'd rather bowl with." Michael looked lovingly down at me, and I felt my stomach do a little flip flop.

"Now, don't go getting soft on me." I punched his shoulder playfully. Because then I might really do something stupid to sabotage our relationship.

"Ruthie, you guys want to play?" Jim asked at the end of the second game.

"Play what?" Ruthie replied.

"Hey, where'd your date go?" Mary asked.

Ruthie looked around as if noticing he was missing for the first time. Then we all spotted him, two lanes down with his face inches from the ball return. The red, belted wheel whizzed dangerously close to his nose.

"He's a bit odd, isn't he?" I whispered to Mary.

"Odd as an aardvark," she replied dryly.

I repeated Mary's words. "You don't mean, like, for real."

Mary raised her eyebrows.

"An aardvark shifter?" That would be a new one.

"Mm-hm." Mary took a sip of her beer.

"That would explain the nose," I said before I could stop myself. I blame the beer.

Mary let out a genuine, honest-to-goodness laugh. I was only sorry that it was at the aardvark's expense.

"Be my maid of honor," Mary blurted out.

"Wait, what?" My eyes were wide with alarm. Where did that come from? We weren't even talking about the wedding. In fact, I could have sworn Mary wasn't even thinking about it.

"Please? Barbara Jean isn't going to be able to, and Michael is the best man. It'll be perfect."

"I ... don't know what to say," I confessed.

"Don't make me ask Ruthie. We're family and all, but she's a little out there." Mary motioned down to the other lane where Ruthie had joined her date in sticking her face too close for comfort to the ball return.

"What's going on?" Jim asked as he and Michael joined the conversation.

"I want Vee to be my maid of honor," Mary replied confidently, her expression brimming with hope.

"Oh, that's a perfect solution, isn't it?" Jim rubbed Mary's back as if it was a done deal.

I visibly swallowed and looked over to Michael to gauge his expression.

"Completely up to you," he said softly so only I could hear above the clamoring of pins behind us. I knew Michael meant it. He wasn't going to pressure me into anything, which was exactly the support I needed.

I exhaled a breath I hadn't even realized I'd been holding. "What do I need to do exactly?" I asked Mary.

She squealed in response, pulling me into a tight embrace.

"Okay, okay, now," I said as Mary held on tight.

"This is going to be great." Mary held me at arm's length and looked at me with tears of happiness pooling in her eyes.

I know I said I wanted to make the bride happy and all. I only hoped I wouldn't make myself miserable in the process.

FIVE

After sleeping in and a late breakfast at the hotel, Michael set off for a White Sox game with the guys.

"Wish it were the Cubbies," Michael said for the umpteenth time.

"I don't because then I'd be jealous." Who cares if the Cub's nineteen sixty-two season was lackluster. Any day at Wriggly Field was a good day.

"Do you think they still have Red Hots?" Michael was a fan of the Chicago-style hot dog with the sesame seed bun and neon green relish.

"It's Chicago, isn't it?"

"I just don't want to get my hopes up."

I laughed on the outside but cringed on the inside. Hot dogs grossed me out even before I became a vegetarian, but for Michael's sake, I hoped he could get his beloved ballpark fare.

"Catch up with you later?" Michael asked with one foot out the door.

"It's a date," I replied.

Thank goodness Mary was fashion-forward and had chosen black bridesmaid dresses, which meant all I had to do was snag an ankle-length black dress, and I was good to go for the ceremony. Now with Michael occupied for the next several hours and with me not having any official maid-of-honor duties until later in the afternoon, it was officially time to start sleuthing.

Pulling the case file out from under the bed, I read everything, including the newspaper clippings, which turned out to be Mrs. Stein and Mr. Compton's obituaries, and decided I would start at the top with the heiress.

It turned out that Mrs. Stein was a patron of the arts, notably the Art Institute of Chicago. The heiress was quoted as saying, "Art gives beauty to life." And she was known to buy the works of more than one local starving artist, which left Mrs. Stein with an impressive art collection, if not in value, then in size. Armed with background knowledge and a list of addresses, I headed out to see if anyone was home at the Stein house.

* * *

Mrs. Stein had lived on the 10th floor in a luxury condo off North Michigan Avenue.

"I'm sorry, but the condo isn't open for showings yet," a middle-aged upper-class woman said when she opened the door to me. Her red hair was set in perfect curls, and a glass of white wine sloshed in her hand. Behind her, framed artwork stood stacked in the foyer, and a collection of moving boxes took up the rest of the space.

"No, that's not what I'm here for," I quickly interjected before the woman could shut the door to dismiss me.

"Don't tell me you're a reporter. I've had enough of those stopping by. Good for nothing. That's what they all are. Can't let a poor woman rest in peace. Have to try and dig up dirt. Disgraceful, that's what it is." The woman downed her wine. "Ahhhh," she sighed, licking her lips.

"I promise, I'm not a reporter."

The woman cocked her head to the side as if she wasn't expecting me to say that. "You're not?"

"Trust me. No one would read anything I wrote." Writing was not my strong suit.

"Then, I'm sorry. Who are you?" The woman went to take another drink before remembering her glass was empty.

"My name is Vee. I knew Mrs. Stein through the

art institute. I came by to express my condolences and see if you needed any help."

The woman scrutinized me. Either that or her eyes were having a hard time focusing. If it was the former, I dressed for the occasion, donning the most business professional ensemble Michael had purchased—a white shirt with an oversized bow collar and little black polka dots paired with black trousers and an emerald green button-up blazer. A small cluster of pearls studded each ear, and my makeup was flawless.

My look must've passed the test if that's what it was. "Well, heaven knows I could use some help here. If you're offering, I can't see any good reason to turn you away." The woman opened the door the rest of the way for me to come in.

Mrs. Stein had one of those condos that your mouth hit the floor as soon as you walked in. The entire west-facing wall of the living room comprised floor-to-ceiling windows, giving a panoramic view of the crystal-blue waters of Lake Michigan. It was breathtaking. Sailboats glided in the distance as seagulls hovered above the sun-glinted water. I could only imagine what the sunsets looked like every evening.

"I can't believe Jill's gone," the woman said, pouring herself another glass of wine from the pristine white kitchen. A long countertop separated the kitchen from the dining area, but the space was open other than that.

"You knew her well?"

"Best friends for over forty years."

If that was true, then I was betting this woman was also a witch or, at the very least, knew supernaturals were real. "I'm sorry. What's your name?" I asked.

"Alice Meyers," the woman replied, taking a hefty drink from her glass. "The world's not going to be the same without Jill."

"That it won't." From the looks of things, Alice was in the process of removing Jill's artwork from the walls and packing it away. She had brown wrapping paper unraveled across the expansive dining room table. A stack of framed photos sat piled up at the head of the table, waiting their turn. I stepped in, taking the brown packing paper and wrapping it tightly around a photograph before sliding it into the slotted box and doing the same with another. Alice continued to drink heavily.

"What do you think happened to her?" I asked, not looking up from my task. When Alice didn't answer, I pressed on. "We saw her at the Institute not more than a day before it happened, looking fit as could be. I can't imagine her passing away like that." This time I did look up to gauge Alice's reaction.

"You're going to think I'm crazy." Alice stared into her empty glass.

"I promise you I won't." I gave the woman my full attention.

"What does it matter now?" Alice asked herself. Seeming to make up her mind, she added, "I think she was murdered."

"You do?"

"I can't explain it. The energy in here is off. Do you believe in magic?" Alice looked up and met my eyes.

"I do." My voice was solemn.

"I'm not talking about parlor tricks," Alice clarified.

"Neither am I." A moment of silence passed between us.

"I think she was cursed. I don't know why or by whom, but I have this intuition, and my intuition is never wrong."

"Any idea who would do such a thing?"

"That's the thing. Everyone loved Jill." Alice's eyes brimmed with tears.

I grabbed a box of tissues and walked over to place them in front of her. The countertop separated us. Alice dabbed the moisture away.

"What about for her money? It's no secret that

she was wealthy. Surely someone would benefit, or could it have been blackmail?"

"Jill would've told me if someone was blackmailing her." Alice poured the rest of the bottle into her glass and downed it. "And her will was locked tight. All of the money is going to area charities. Everyone knows Jill had a soft spot for lost causes." Alice said the last part to herself.

I wondered how desperate these lost causes were and how to find out. Wills were usually private until the person passed away and the estate filed the document with probate court; that's how it worked in modern times. But who knew when that would be, and I didn't have time to waste. Alice swayed on her feet, and I knew it would only be a matter of minutes before the alcohol entirely went to her head.

"Have you read her will? Because if you're right, a charity beneficiary could've killed her."

"Hm?" Alice's eyes fluttered shut, and I raced around the counter to catch her before she hit the ground.

Alice slumped into my arms. I struggled to support her as we made our way to the living room. Alice's head was dead weight on my shoulder. Her feet dragged on the carpet, leaving a trail in our wake. *No more donuts,* I thought to myself as I struggled with Alice's weight, which wasn't an insult to her as much as it was to myself. *But donuts are so good*, the other half of my conscience argued. We stumbled along. *Okay, not as many donuts then.*

"OOF!" I plopped Alice as gracefully as possible onto the sofa. She slightly stirred while I fussed, pulling an afghan off a nearby chair and tucking her in.

"Thank you," Alice said, closing her eyes and smacking her tongue on the roof of her mouth.

I fetched a glass and filled it with water, putting it beside her on the end table so it would be within reach when she woke. Alice rolled over onto her side, so her back faced the sofa and drifted off to sleep.

I didn't waste any time searching for Mrs. Stein's will.

In addition to the kitchen, dining room, and living room, the apartment also boasted two bedrooms, each with ensuites and another guest bath. If there had been a home office, I would've started my search there, but seeing there wasn't, I thought the master bedroom would be my best shot at finding the document.

Thankfully, I didn't have to search alone. My magic always had my back. Mrs. Stein had one of those beds that I've always read about in romance novels but I've never actually seen. The king-size four-poster bed made a statement, dominating the entire room. The frame was rich mahogany, contrasting perfectly with the white chiffon fabric she had draped across the top and cascaded loosely down the sides. Beyond the bed was a sliding glass door that opened to a balcony offering an unobstructed view of the water below.

I stood at the foot of the bed and closed my eyes, taking a deep breath to center myself. In my mind, I pictured the document I was looking for. I imagined the words The Last Will and Testament scrolled across the top of the page. With the document visualized, I whispered the words:

Heaven and Earth, I call thee,
show me the document I long to see,
Jill Stein's will is what I need,
to solve this case, please make haste.

For a moment, I only heard the ticking of a bedside clock, keeping time with my heartbeat, but then I felt it—a soft tug at my solar plexus. I opened my eyes and stood, then walked toward Mrs. Stein's tall dresser but stopped when I was still two steps away. That direction wasn't right. I stood still for a moment, waiting to be pulled in the right direction, and found myself backtracking toward the closet. I put my hand on the doorknob and shook my head. That wasn't right, either. Was the document in her nightstand? Again, that felt right for a second, but I quickly realized that too was wrong. My internal compass was spinning wild and making me dizzy in the process. It took me a minute to figure out what was going on. And then it hit me. The document had been enchanted, protected if you will, from prying eyes. Jill hadn't wanted anyone to find it.

That meant I was going to have to focus harder. I opened the sliding door and let the fresh air clear the confusion from my head. The wind was strong this high up and being on the water. The gauzy fabric surrounding the bed blew back, and the soft wisps of my hair did the same. I sat on the edge of the bed, letting the wind move through me, and dug my hands into the thick, white comforter. With fistfuls of the fabric, I reached out to the universe.

"I wish her no harm," I whispered. "I only want to give her peace. Please help me." In my mind, I envisioned my power shooting out from the center of my chest, sending my message into the atmosphere to Jill, asking for her blessing.

For several minutes, nothing happened—only more ticking from the alarm clock and my heart.

Then, slowly from below me, the bed grew warm as if I was sitting on a heated blanket. At first, I thought it was coming from me, but as the heat increased, I knew it was another supernatural force at play. I got down off the bed, lifted the skirt, and peered underneath. Jill had boxes stacked under the bed along with more paintings and something else. A slim, tan metal box glowed a warm honey color. Cautiously, I reach out, checking the box's surrounding temperature. I didn't want to get burned. The ward allowed me to pass through without incident. I placed my hands on the metal box and slid it out from underneath the bed. It had a flip-top lid similar to what you would see on a safe deposit box, right down to the circular lock. Thankfully, I didn't need a key. Picking locks was my specialty.

I placed my fingers on the lock and once again closed my eyes. In my mind, I pictured inserting a key into the slot. As the tumblers aligned, I turned the invisible key in my head and released the latch. The lock released with a soft pop.

The document was placed right on top, sitting on a stack of other papers, including the deed to the apartment, Mrs. Stein's birth certificate, a handful of black-and-white photos, and miscellaneous mementos collected over a lifetime. Items such as ticket stubs, theater programs, birthday cards. I read through the will and noted with surprise that she had updated it days before her death, leaving a large portion of her fortune, ten million dollars, to The Future Is Tomorrow Coalition.

"Who in the world are they?" I pondered aloud. Ten million in nineteen sixty-two was over eighty million in today's dollars. That's a lot of dollar bills.

The rest of the beneficiaries were what I expected. Places like the Chicago Art Institute, the opera house, neighborhood theater clubs, and a small stipend for the artist in residence at a local university. I placed the document back in the box, relocked it with my magic, and safely tucked it away.

Before leaving the apartment, I checked in on Alice one last time and found that she was still sleeping away. Rest was the best thing for the poor woman. Because when she woke up, she was going to have one heck of a hangover.

SIX

I decided to wait on researching The Future Is Tomorrow Coalition, as that would eat into my morning, and I still wanted to interview Bernie's family and Xavier, the vampire hunter, and check in on Barbara Jean. I didn't have an address for Xavier, so I was hoping he was still in the hospital since his attack had been recent.

But first up was Bernie. His apartment building wasn't too far from Mrs. Stein's in location but a world away in terms of luxury. The three-story red brick unit lacked a doorman and elevator, but it did retain some charm in the potted geraniums out front and freshly painted foyer. On one side of the wall were a series of locked, metal mailboxes recessed into the wall. On the opposite wall was a door with a sign that read laundry. A split-second decision told me to check out the crime scene before interviewing Bernie's widow.

Opening the wooden door revealed a series of steps that only went down. Teal-green linoleum lined the stairs and landing. The walls were unpainted cinder blocks, and the natural lighting was nonexistent. A set of three washers and three dryers lined opposite walls with a wooden folding table set up in the center. A couple of metal folding chairs stood propped up against the wall. I flicked on the overhead light, illuminating the cobwebs in the corner. I brushed at the invisible spider I felt crawling up my neck and shrieked when I realized it hadn't been my imagination after all. The little black arachnoid scurried across the floor, disappearing under a dryer. I did a little heebie-jeebie dance at the thought of any of his little buddies still crawling on me.

"Are you okay?" A smooth voice asked from the doorway. The woman held her tight, black corkscrew curls back with a red bandana, and she had a basket of clothes tucked under her brown-toned arm.

"Yeah, sorry. Spider."

"You get used to them down here," the young woman replied, walking in the rest of the way and setting her laundry basket down on the table. "You new in the building?" she asked while sorting out her loads.

"Not exactly."

The woman looked up and met my eyes. Something about her features was familiar, but I didn't know what. I tried not to stare and quickly realized she was waiting on me to elaborate.

"I'm looking into Mr. Compton's death."

"Cop?"

"More like a private investigator."

"I see. Well, it's awful that man died down here. Can you imagine the last thing you ever see is this dingy place? And to die all alone?" She shook her head.

"I agree. It is awful." I paused for a minute. "How well did you know Mr. Compton?"

"If you're asking if I was friendly with him, that's a big, fat no. But then again, no one was. The man kept to himself unless he was accusing you of stealing his soap." The woman pointed to the cabinet against the wall.

"Not the friendliest of guys," I summarized.

"Not by a long shot. You thinking someone murdered him?" The woman looked around the basement ominously.

"Right now, I don't know how he died, but it's possible."

The woman nodded as if rethinking her plans.

"Do you know Mr. Compton's wife? Gloria, I believe?" That was the name listed in the obituary.

The woman's eyes got wide. "You don't want to talk to her."

"That bad?"

"Why do you think Mr. Compton sat down here in this damp, dark basement and did his laundry alone? Even he couldn't stand her. The fights those two had. If he was murdered, half the complex would point the finger at her. The other half just haven't lived here long enough."

We were both silent for a minute.

"You don't think something down here could've killed him, do you?" the woman asked.

I scanned the seemingly ordinary basement. If I hadn't known better, I'd never known that a man died down here. The police hadn't left a grim chalk outline or a strip of crime scene tape anywhere. And it wasn't like management had posted anything on the laundry room door. As far as they and the police were concerned, it was business as usual, and Bernie's death wasn't under investigation. I knew better.

"I honestly don't know. But if I were you, I'd find someplace else to do my laundry until we can get this sorted out." I didn't think the killer was still lurking, but I didn't know that for sure. For all I knew, the killer lived in the building, or maybe they bewitched the washing machine. Stranger things have happened.

"You don't have to tell me twice." The woman tossed her laundry back into the basket and tucked it underneath her arm. "I was thinking about taking a walk anyway." I held the door open for her to walk out with me.

We parted ways on the ground floor, the woman walking to the end of the hall to enter her apartment and me heading up one flight of stairs to the Compton residence. My knuckles hadn't even made contact with the door before a woman was yanking it open and pointing her finger in my face.

"What do you want?" she snapped and then sniffed the air around me. Her blue and pink patterned housecoat swayed above her knees. "We don't need any witches around here," she growled, not even attempting to hide her otherworldliness.

I decided not to beat around the bush. "Gloria Compton?"

"What do you want?" she snapped at me.

"My name is Vee Harper. I am investigating a string of suspicious attacks, and I wanted to talk to you about your husband's death."

"You're a reporter for that stupid newspaper, aren't you? I can tell you one thing, my husband wasn't scared to death. He had nerves of steel. It would take more than a ghost to rattle him."

"I agree. That's why I'm here. I think there's more going on than what the newspapers reported."

"And it concerns you how?" The shifter glared at me with ice in her eyes.

"Because this is my community, and it seems that none of us are safe."

"You're a cop, aren't you? I can smell it."

I sniffed my arm and wondered if the Bureau had a spray I could use to block the scent of authority. I went with the same lie I'd told the woman downstairs and said, "Private investigator, but I promise you that I just want the best for the neighborhood."

The woman eyed me suspiciously but still opened the door for me to enter. Inside, a nicotine haze filled the air courtesy of the cigarette burning in the nearby ashtray on the coffee table. The ash was easily two inches long. Instead of picking up that cigarette, the woman dug another one out of her housecoat and lit it. She took a seat on the rust-colored couch, and I copied her move, sitting on the opposite side. My eyes stung from the amount of cigarette smoke in the air, and I had a feeling the cream-colored walls were painted a bright white under their coat of tar.

"The man died of a heart attack. End of story,"

she said on the exhale, blowing smoke right in my face.

I waved the smoke away. "You believe that?"

"And why shouldn't I? Bernie had a bad heart. Trucking those laundry baskets up and down the stairs every week. It was only a matter of time."

"Do you know he wasn't the only person found that way?"

"So the newspaper says. But who can believe that trash?"

"And yet you invited me in."

Mrs. Compton took a long draw off of her cigarette. I pressed on.

"Do you know anyone that would want to hurt your husband?"

The woman barked out a laugh. "Do you know what my husband did for a living? Who didn't want him dead? He had a hand in everything, that man."

"I thought your husband was retired?"

"Next question." Mrs. Compton tapped her cigarette in the ashtray.

"Did you or your husband know Jill Stein?"

"Do I look like I was buddy-buddy with that rich witch? That's me, best friends with an heiress. This is just our summer home." Gloria motioned to the relatively small living room and barked out a laugh, which became a coughing fit complete with wheezing. I wanted to tell her to lay off the smokes, but I held my tongue.

"You're not very good at your job, are you?" The shifter's laugh continued, punctuated with coughs.

"Does The Future Is Tomorrow Coalition ring a bell for you?" I asked.

"Get out."

"Excuse me?"

"I said, get out. Now." Mrs. Compton flicked her cigarette in the air. It landed in the ashtray.

"I don't know anything about them. One of the other victims—"

"You got fur in your ears? Get out!"

"If you could tell me who they are or where they're located."

Mrs. Compton raised her hand to silence me, and I saw that she had begun to shift. Claws and tufts of gray fur met my eyes. I stood and backed up slowly. The last thing I wanted was to take on a full-fledged wolf.

"I'll just be going," I said, backtracking to the door. "If you change your mind and want to talk, I'm at The Duke hotel through the weekend."

Gloria glowered at me through the smoke in the air. I offered up the friendliest smile I could muster and said goodbye.

SEVEN

Well, that escalated quickly, I thought as I hailed a cab and headed to Mercy General. Hopefully, Xavier would be more cooperative, and maybe he'd know a thing or two about the coalition and, more importantly, be willing to talk. That is if he was still a patient at Mercy General. If not, I'd have to put a call out to the Bureau and see if they could track him down or give me a lead. In the meantime, I could still check up on Barbara Jean and ask her a few questions if she was up for it. I hadn't witnessed anything unusual in the moments leading to her supernatural assault, but maybe her heightened senses picked up something.

The cab dropped me off in the circular drive, and I walked inside. One thing was for sure: it didn't matter what year you were in, hospitals still smelled the same. I walked up to the front desk and asked the receptionist to help me locate Xavier James.

The older woman didn't look up but instead focused on her clipboard. "Afraid I can't do that," she finally said after flipping through a couple of pages.

"What? Why not?" I tried peering over the counter at the papers. "Was he released?"

The receptionist hugged the clipboard tightly to her chest and glared up at me. "It says no visitors," she said matter-of-factly.

"Was that by his request or hospital policy?"

"I assume his."

"Oh, well, I'm sure he'd want to see me. I'm his sister," I countered with the first lie that came to mind.

"If he wanted to see you, it wouldn't say no visitors next to his name, now would it?"

"True, but he didn't know I was in town. And we're very close. I know he'd be very upset if you turned me away, and I'm sure you wouldn't want that. So, is there any chance you can help me out?" I smiled encouragingly, hoping the woman would relent and give me the room number if anything to get me out of her hair.

"I'm afraid I can't help you."

"But this is important. I need to speak to him. It's an emergency."

"Again, it says no visitors."

"I understand that, but if you could just give me a minute with him, or perhaps deliver a note? I'm sure it doesn't say no mail." Again, I tried to peer at the clipboard.

The receptionist glanced behind me. I followed her gaze to the security station, where a guard was on standby. She opened her mouth to call him over, and my magical instincts kicked in. I reached out and touched the woman's wrist.

"Hey!" was all she managed to get out before I sent a shot of volts from my body straight into hers. The woman's eyes rolled back, and I counted to two before letting go.

"Let me help you with that," I offered, taking the clipboard from her and flipping through the pages until I stopped at the J's. The woman sat stunned, which was exactly what I wanted. My finger ran down the list of patient names and room numbers, stopping when I found Xavier James. He was in room 527. I then flipped to the next page, where I located Barbara Jean's name. She was on the third floor, room 313.

"Excellent. Thank you." I handed the clipboard back. "Maybe you should take a five-minute break. Get a cup of coffee or take a walk outside. It's beautiful out." I motioned to the sunlight filtering in through the hospital's expansive front windows.

"Coffee. Break. Yeah, that does sound nice."

"Doesn't it? And I do appreciate your help. I can tell that you take your job very seriously. I'm sure the hospital is thankful to have a worker like you." The woman smiled in a dazed sort of way. I patted my hand twice on the counter, signaling my goodbye and helping to snap the woman out of it, and headed off to the elevators.

The elevator seemed to take forever, stopping at each floor as visitors and hospital personnel hopped on and off. I moved further and further to the back as more people joined us on the third floor. Then when we reached the fourth floor, we were all asked to step off so the hospital could transfer a patient. I willingly obliged, exiting last and hoofing it to the nearest staircase. Thankfully it was merely feet away. I yanked open the heavy, ivory-painted metal door and readily took to the cement steps. I should've taken the stairs in the first place, I thought.

It was a good thing I got there when I did because Xavier was one minute away from walking out the door. I walked in as he tugged down a plain white T-shirt over his sandy blond tousled hair. A dark brown leather coat sat beside him on the bed. The young man looked rough. His skin was pale, and dark circles showed through his warm complexion. You could tell that his skin tone was the type that tanned easily. Lucky guy. When it came to the sun, I was either pale or burnt, with no in-between, which made me thankful I could glamour makeup when the situation warranted it.

"You getting out of here?" I asked. It was a rhetorical question.

"I've had enough fun for one lifetime. Give the doc my best, will you?" Xavier grabbed his coat and went to walk out the door.

"Hold up. I don't work here."

"Then I definitely don't want to talk to you." Xavier went to brush past me.

"Ouch."

"No offense. Places to go. People to see."

"Vampires to hunt," I threw out there. That stopped him in his tracks. He looked over his shoulder at me from the doorway. "Yes, I know who you are."

Xavier reached in his pocket for heaven only knows what, and I held my hand up in an offensive position. I was ready to blast him one.

"Don't even try me, buddy. I only wanted to ask you a couple of questions."

"You've got thirty seconds." Xavier crossed his arms and leaned against the door jamb.

"What can you tell me about the attack?"

"This?" Xavier pointed at his chest. "Can you even call it that?"

"Something happened to you."

Xavier shrugged his shoulders.

"Listen, you're not the only one who's been stunned, cursed, or whatever you want to call it. I'm trying to figure out who's behind it, and I need your help."

"Who says it's related?"

"Call it a hunch."

"Well, I don't know what happened. One minute I was working out at the gym, and the next thing I know, I'm here."

"And doesn't that bother you?"

"Do you know how many people have tried to kill me?"

"I'm betting a lot."

"Too many."

"You could always change careers."

"So could you." Xavier stared me down, and I returned the look. There was something supernatural about him, but I wasn't sure what. I wasn't getting the witch vibe or even the scent of a shifter, but he was something. The fact that he was the only one walking after being stunned and now calling me out said as much. It must be the vampire blood.

I sighed in frustration, feeling like I wasn't getting anywhere. "Listen, you obviously know your supes. Were your senses tripped beforehand?"

"No, but if I had a dollar for every time someone cursed me, I wouldn't need to do what I do."

"So, you do think you were cursed."

Xavier shrugged his shoulders again. "Anything else?"

"How long are you in town for?" Vampire hunters never stayed in one area. It was an occupational hazard.

"I've already been here too long." Xavier turned and walked the rest of the way out of the room.

"Wait," I called after him in the hallway. Xavier stopped and looked over his shoulder. "Does The Future Is Tomorrow Coalition mean anything to you?"

"Never heard of them," he replied without looking back. And just like that, Xavier James walked away.

I wasn't sure what to make of Xavier. I bypassed the elevators and headed down two flights to Barbara Jean's room. The scenes between the two rooms were strikingly different. Where Xavier's curtains had been open and the room bright, Barbara Jean had her shades drawn and the lighting dim.

I was also struck by how different hospital

rooms are today compared to nineteen sixty-two. There were no machines. Nothing was beeping or blooping on a screen. A glass IV bottle hung upside down from a pole, and a large green canister stood beside the bed, giving Barbara Jean a steady supply of fluid and oxygen. Over at the sink, instead of a wall-mounted container of hand soap, there was a bright green bottle of something called Phisohex, and just looking at the soap substitute made my skin itch.

Honestly, the scene was far too quiet and sterile for my liking. I'd rather face the likes of Xavier than walk into a somber situation. I had to let go of my frustration with the vampire hunter and quickly switched gears to one of compassion.

I didn't see the young girl right away. Balled up in a chair, tucked in the corner, the girl looked at me. Her dark doe eyes were questioning, waiting for me to say something.

"I'm Vee, a friend of Mary's," I whispered. "How is she?" The young girl shrugged. I walked further into the room. "Are you Barbara Jean's sister?"

The girl nodded.

"I heard your mom said she was going to be okay." The young girl watched me hesitantly. "Is your mom by chance here?"

The girl shook her head. "She had to go home

and feed my brothers." I had to lean forward to hear her.

"Oh, you have brothers?"

"Lots of 'em."

"You poor girl."

The young girl smiled at my comment. "They drive Mama crazy. She says they're worse than a pack of wolves."

"Does she now?" Guess that meant Barbara Jean wasn't a wolf shifter. "Has Barbara Jean been awake more?"

"She just sleeps. But I'm supposed to call the nurse if she wakes." The young girl seemed to repeat the instructions from her mama word for word.

I looked down at Barbara Jean. She lay motionless. A white blanket was pulled taut across her waist, leaving her arms straight down at her sides, giving the nurses unobstructed access to her IV. It was impossible to tell if she was even breathing. Her chest wasn't moving even though a nasal cannula provided a steady stream of oxygen. I resisted the urge to check her pulse, trusting that the doctors and nurses knew what they were doing.

I changed my focus, "What about you? Can I get you anything? A pop or candy bar?" I was almost positive I saw a vending machine out in the hallway.

"I'm okay, thanks."

"Are you sure?" I dug in my purse for some change regardless and handed over two dimes and a nickel, enough for more than one snack.

"Thank you," the young girl mumbled into the coins.

"You're very welcome. Now when your sister wakes up, tell her we're all thinking of her. Okay?"

"Okay," she replied, disappearing into the chair once again.

I stood there a minute longer, wanting to offer up words of encouragement or promises that Barbara Jean would be okay, but instead only gave the young girl a soft smile and a wave goodbye.

EIGHT

As I stepped outside, I wanted nothing more than to continue sleuthing, but wedding duties called, and I was still determined to make Mary's wedding dreams come true. Tonight was a formal cocktail party hosted by the bride's family, the Rigattis. Michael said it was to welcome all of the wedding guests into town and kick off the weekend festivities.

"Is there an itinerary somewhere?" I joked with Michael once back at the hotel and in my formal wear. It seemed something was planned every day from here on out. Sometimes multiple things. I checked myself out in the floor-length mirror, deciding to wear the red, tea-length cocktail dress Michael had picked out. With a sweetheart neckline and capped sleeves, it might be my favorite dress yet. I could definitely wear it in either decade.

"Actually, I think there is." Michael opened his suitcase and rifled through it, looking for the itinerary, but came up empty. He went to look in the nightstand drawer, and I stopped him short, knowing I had stashed the case file there.

"Never mind, it's not a big deal. As long as you know where we need to be, it's all good." I quickly turned Michael's shoulders, so he was facing me and worked on fixing his tie. I adjusted the length of the satiny gray-striped material and tightened the knot under his neck before turning down his crisp white shirt collar and brushing lint off his sport coat.

"I like this look on you. Navy is your color."

"And red is yours." Michael looked down at me. His expression was smoldering. I felt tingly all the way down to my toes, and it had nothing to do with the high heels I was wearing.

I cleared my throat. "We better get out of here before you make us late." I walked over to the door and looked over my shoulder with a wink.

The cocktail reception was to take place in The Duke's formal ballroom. On the way down, I cast a quick cloaking spell over Michael and me before we walked in. A proactive mental bubble, if you will. The move was more for our sanity than anything else. Everyone there was a supernatural, and being around that much energy was sure to make us both a bit crazy. You could bet I would take advantage of whatever magic I could do to stymie that.

"I'm going to guess that Mary likes yellow?" I said as we entered the ballroom. There was yellow decor everywhere, including yellow tablecloths, napkins, and roses. The cheery blooms served as centerpieces and were pinned to the lapels of the waitstaff's uniforms.

"There's Mary's parents, Vito and Antonia," Michael said, pointing to a couple greeting guests as they arrived. Even the Rigattis ensemble coordinated with the decor. Mr. Rigatti, with his short stature and plump midsection, had donned an off-white tux that could've passed as a pale shade of yellow, and Mrs. Rigatti wore an off-the-shoulder yellow satin dress. The bright hue tied in nicely with the rich blue carpet and golden tapestries in the room. With dark wood paneling and expansive crystal chandeliers, the whole room looked quite regal.

"And those are Jim's parents, Stan and Sally Wilson," Michael said, pointing to the uncomfortable couple standing off to the side. Stan wore tan dress pants and loafers, and Sally wore a floral house dress. The missus' hair was an uncontrolled frizz, and her wrists were heavy with bangles and turquoise.

"Heck of a potions witch," Michael murmured.

"Really?"

"If you need a draught drawn up, she's your witch."

I nodded and filed the information away for later.

The room was packed as guests mingled about, sipping from their highballs and champagne flutes. A pianist played a soft jazz tune on the stage, the notes barely registering over the chatter and laughter.

Michael eyed the bar in the corner. "Cocktail?"

"That'd be great. I'll go look for Jim and Mary."

Michael and I parted ways as I walked further into the crowded room. However, I didn't make it very far before Nancy found me.

"Vee, there you are. I wondered if you were going to be here tonight. I heard the exciting news. Congrats!" the newspaper editor exclaimed.

"What? What news? I'm not following." I eyed Nancy suspiciously and then looked about the room for a clue.

"That you're the maid of honor, silly." Nancy waved her hand in the air.

"Oh, that news. Yeah. I thought ... I don't know."

"Wait, are you pregnant?" Nancy shouted. Several heads swiveled in our direction.

"What! No! Not at all. No." I shook my head vehemently.

"There I go again, blurting things out. Don't mind me. False alarm," Nancy said over her shoulder.

Once again, everyone heard her. She then leaned in and whispered, "But seriously, are you?"

"No!" This time I was the one doing the shouting.

"Okay, okay. I can't help it. I'm always looking for the scoop."

"Speaking of which, where's your camera?"

"What? Oh. No, I'm here tonight as an official guest. My family and the Wilsons go way back. I've known Jim since we were in diapers." Nancy laughed. "My mother's around here somewhere." Nancy scanned the room but apparently didn't find her.

Michael joined us at that moment. "That was fast,"I said, taking my amaretto sour from his hand.

"Prompt service," he replied, taking a sip of his drink.

"Michael, this is Nancy. A family friend of Jim's," I said by way of introduction.

"Nice to meet you, Nancy." Michael shook her hand.

"You're a cop, aren't you?" She shot back.

"Ah," Michael looked to me for help, but he was all on his own. I smiled and took a drink. "A detective, yes." Michael tucked his free hand in his pocket and nodded.

"Thought so. You give off that authoritative vibe.

A real rule follower." Nancy turned to me. "Her, not so much."

Michael chuckled.

"You believe in freedom of the press?" Nancy pressed on to Michael.

"Sure, absolutely," he replied.

"See, we need more officers like you," Nancy said. "Members of law enforcement who understand the press have an important role to play. The people deserve to know what's happening in their city!" Nancy continued on her tangent, going on about the importance of honest and timely news.

"Nancy's a local newspaper editor," I supplied, answering the bewildered expression on Michael's face.

"Got it," he replied as if that explained it.

"Yes, the Midnight Express. Have you heard of it?" Nancy asked.

"Not yet. But I'm sure I will. And speaking of being timely, there's Mary and Jim. We should probably say hi," Michael said to me.

"Yes, you're right. We should. It was nice seeing you again," I said to Nancy.

"Nice meeting you," Michael added.

"Likewise," Nancy replied with a finger salute.

Michael and I started walking away when I stopped short. I had planned on looking up The

Future Is Tomorrow Coalition in the phone book and see if they had a physical address, but maybe Nancy knew something about them.

"You go on ahead. I'll catch up with you," I said to Michael, backtracking to catch up with Nancy.

"Hey, long time no see," Nancy joked.

"Aren't you funny. Listen, I have a question. I heard a couple of people talking about this organization, a coalition of sorts. I was wondering if you've heard anything about it?" I was careful about how I worded my question, knowing Nancy would run with any information I gave her. It would be a headline before I knew it. And the last thing I wanted was for my lead to get tipped off.

"What's it called?"

"The Future Is Tomorrow—"

"Shut your mouth," Nancy hissed, slapping her hand over my lips.

I pulled my head back. "What in the world?"

Nancy grabbed me by the wrist and dragged me out of the ballroom.

"What is with everybody?" I asked as we walked out into the hotel lobby.

"How far are you from out of town anyway, the moon?"

Oh, further away than that, I thought.

"The Future Is Tomorrow Coalition is the shell

company for the Rigattis," Nancy said under her breath.

"As in the bride's family."

"Right. And one of Chicago's most powerful crime families."

"Oh," I breathed, my mouth making a perfect round O shape. "Mafia?" I whispered.

Nancy nodded her head solemnly. "Who was talking about it?"

"What?"

"The coalition. Who was talking about it? It wasn't anyone here, was it?"

"You know, I can't even remember," I lied. "But now I know it's none of my business, I'll be sure to steer clear of any crime family conversations. Thanks." I turned on my heel and walked briskly away, not looking over my shoulder.

But when I walked back into the ballroom, I stopped short.

Standing stage center was the same young woman from the laundry room this afternoon. Edith Adams. Her name popped right into my head.

"She's got some pipes on her, don't she?" an older shifter said from beside me. Edith was crooning a beautiful ballad accompanied by a jazz quintet.

That's why she looked so familiar. Edith Adams would go on to become a jazz legend, winning at least half-a-dozen Grammys and selling millions of records. I got goosebumps standing there, listening to her sing.

Michael met me once more. "Care to dance?"

"Love to." I turned to set my cocktail down, and Michael grabbed me by the hand. I assumed he would lead me out to the crowded dance floor, but instead, we found a quiet corner and danced alone together in the shadows. My stomach felt jittery, and I realized I was nervous. Make that guilty too. The two emotions sat like weights on my chest. I knew it was because I was keeping the case from Michael. That was the only explanation.

"Nice to slow down every now and then, isn't it?" he asked.

"What? Absolutely. Yes. I love slowing down. It's the best." Even I didn't believe the words coming out of my mouth.

Michael looked down at me. His eyebrow raised quizzically. That got a nervous laugh out of me. I cleared my throat and thought now was as good a time as any to tell Michael about the case. If the mafia truly was involved, I would need all the help I could get. Michael was a good detective. We'd partnered together on cases in the past and could do it again. I only had to get over the guilt of wrecking his weekend.

"Well, you see ... it's just that after we got here. How did it start? Ah, you remember when I went to the bakery? When I met Mary? Well—"

Magical gold sparks shot out from the dance floor, interrupting my confession. They zigzagged across the ballroom like rogue fireworks, causing guests to scream and run for cover. Shouting ensued, and insults flew, followed by more magical sparks, this time purple and green. The mayhem centered around two women fighting in the center of the dance floor. Around us, the air shimmered, and electricity hummed. The chandeliers and wall sconces power surged in response, their bulbs brightening to dangerous levels. Energy ripped through the room, popping my cloaking bubble with it. Without a shield, the force of the power in the ballroom hit me full center. I couldn't breathe as all-out magical warfare broke out. Sparks and curses rang out as clothing tore, and animal calls pierced the air from the shifters morphing in plain sight. No one cowered. Everyone was fighting. I even spotted a sloth throwing cream puffs from the top of the curtains. Although, I'm not sure how effective they were, lobbing one pastry a minute.

"Holy cats!" I shouted.

"And wolves too," Michael quipped.

A pack of wolf pups—I think they were the

bride's little cousins—ran amok, turning over the dessert table and crashing into the waitstaff in front of us. I jumped back, but not fast enough. In an instant, my dress was covered in cannoli cream. Meatballs and sauce splattered down the front of Michael's white dress shirt. The shrimp tartlets and antipasti kebabs missed us by inches and now littered the floor. Miniature mozzarella balls, cherry tomatoes, and black olives were pulverized into the carpet. I had to sidestep to avoid squashing a tomato and a rat.

"What the heck! Where did that come from?" I exclaimed as the rodent ran between my legs, just missing biting my ankle with its elongated yellow teeth.

"Now that's a rat," Michael replied as the extra-large black rat ran across the ballroom floor.

Another scream rang out, and Michael and I sprang into action. In a regular fight, one would expect people to flee the chaos, but that wasn't the case with supernaturals. Once the guests realized they weren't in danger, anger replaced fear. A line was drawn, shifters versus witches, leaving Jim and Mary in the center of it all.

Tables flipped, and glass shattered. Roses fell to the floor, creating a slippery scene of water, glass, and foliage as supernaturals battled it out. I ducked as a curse flew over my head and hit a wolf behind me. The animal immediately began sneezing incessantly, shaking his massive head and sending snot flying. I put my forearm up to block the stray spray when a lightbulb shattered overhead. Shards of glass rained down. I ducked my head and wondered if Michael and I were strong enough to join forces and send out an electrical current to knock everyone down and blast them back to their senses.

Perhaps if they were regular humans, we would've been able to.

I made it to the center of the room where the sparks had erupted to find Dotty, the stuck-up wife of the Pearson duo, locked in a heated battle with a white wolf. The shifter was snarling and snapping while Dotty used sparks to try and set the wolf's fur on fire. She was a nasty witch, firing spell after spell. I'd never seen anything like it.

Mary tried to pull Dotty away and got caught in the crossfire. A random spark flew into her updo, and, POOF, just like that, her hair caught on fire. Mary screamed, running around, inadvertently fanning the flame, making it jump higher. Jim grabbed her a second later and doused his bride's hair with a cocktail, extinguishing the fire and soaking her lace dress.

"This is madness!" I shouted to Michael, turning

around rapidly and throwing out my own electrical force field to stop an approaching fox from nipping my heels.

Then, from the back of the room came a deafening roar of a lion. The sound froze me faster than any spell ever could. The entire ballroom fell to silence, and the fighting ceased immediately. I did not doubt that the lion was Mr. Rigatti. There was a reason lions were called the king of the jungle. His presence demanded the utmost respect. Witches and shifters alike bowed to his will.

I was speechless as the four-hundred-pound cat prowled down the center of the ballroom. The supernaturals parted faster than Moses at the Red Sea. I tore my eyes away from Mr. Rigatti and looked at the guests. Their clothes were torn. Men's ties were ripped off. Tufts of fur were clumped on the floor. Women were missing high heels, and some of their slips were even showing. Not to mention the disaster that was now the decor. Without a word, the shifters began morphing back and started righting the room. The witches followed suit, although more than one of them required medical attention, Michael included.

"Your face is bleeding," I said to him as I picked up a yellow tablecloth. Glass fragments cascaded onto the floor like deadly confetti.

Michael touched the claw marks that ran across

his cheek and down onto his neck. "They're not deep."

I winced on his behalf. I didn't care what he said. They looked like they stung.

Michael paused with his hand to his cheek and closed his eyes. Within seconds his fingertips emitted a faint warm light, and the skin underneath them began to heal. Before my eyes, the cuts closed, becoming puffy pink scars, before fading. A set of four thin, white lines was all that remained.

"Have I ever told you how thankful I am for your sister?" Michael's sister had insisted he learn how to heal after becoming a police officer. Her husband too. She said it helped her sleep better at night, knowing they could keep themselves in one piece.

Michael replied with a half-smile that didn't reach his eyes. I was about to ask him if he was okay when he motioned to the room. "I'm really getting tired of this. One weekend. That's all I wanted. A break from crime and violence. A vacation with my girl. Was that really too much to ask for?"

"No. No, it wasn't," And with that, I knew I'd be keeping the case secret for the rest of the trip.

NINE

After the excitement that night, it took me hours to fall asleep. Michael, not so much. He conked right out, his chest rising and falling in slow, measured breaths. If I hadn't known better, I'd think the man had taken a sleeping tonic. But Michael was gifted that way. He could fall asleep anywhere at any time, the lucky warlock. Me? I lay awake, staring at the popcorn ceiling, wondering why a wealthy witch would leave a fortune to a mafia shifter family. I figured maybe Bernie slipped up somehow and was expendable. But then what about Xavier and Barbara Jean? Where did they fit in? My plot had too many holes, and I didn't like it.

The next morning, I needed a strong cup of coffee, and I looked like it. My short hair was plastered to the side of my head like a crooked mohawk styled with super glue. It was hard to tell where my black eyeliner ended, and the circles under my eyes started. I wasn't one to regularly use glamour. I was more of a "what you see is what you get," but drastic times called for drastic measures, so a little magical makeup was in order.

With my appearance fixed, I was ready to step out of the bathroom and tackle the coffee situation.

A knock came at the door just as I walked past it, but Michael was at the ready.

"I got it," he said. I stood aside as Michael opened the door, and a waiter rolled in a small table with a pristine white cloth.

"Where would you like it?" the waiter asked the two of us.

"By the window would be great," Michael replied.

I watched the waiter maneuver the table toward the window and then reach below it, raising one leaf and then the other, creating a perfect circle. He then removed the metal covers from the dishes and turned to us with a bow. Michael tipped the man, and I moved in for a closer look. Fresh fruit, thick slices of French toast, fresh whipping cream, and a large carafe of coffee awaited. "Bless you," I kissed Michael on the cheek. He smiled and adjusted his shirt.

"Aren't you going to join me?" Michael looked like he was ready to walk out the door.

"Can't. Jim called. It's all hands on deck. Frank's wife, Dotty, started the fight last night. She claims a shifter insulted her shoes."

"So, she started a supernatural war? That woman is such a pill." Images of the woman going nuts last night with her fire spell came to mind.

"You have no idea."

I raised my eyebrows.

"She's insisting the Rigattis pay her for emotional damage," Michael said.

"Are you kidding me? Did she see Mr. Rigatti last night?"

"And," Michael continued, "She's threatening to sue the hotel unless they refund her the room, plus a hundred dollars."

"What does the hotel have to do with it?"

"She's also forbidden Frank from speaking to Jim ever again."

"Now you have to be joking. Is the woman that insecure?" That was the only reason I could think of to explain her behavior. She had to isolate Frank before he realized she was the problem.

"The worst part is that Frank agreed. He's checking out now. And Jim doesn't know what to do. On the one hand, Dotty almost ruined his wedding, but on the other, he doesn't want to lose his friendship with Frank."

I exhaled. Suddenly the food didn't look so appealing. "What about Mary?" Visions of her standing next to Jim with a maraschino cherry and orange slice stuck in her ruined hair came to mind. I wanted to get back to the case, but not if Mary needed me.

"She's at the salon with her mother."

"The poor woman."

"Jim said it's not as bad as it looked. It was mostly the hairspray that went up in flames."

I nodded but still felt awful for her.

"Meet up with you this afternoon?" Michael asked.

"What time's the rehearsal?"

"Three o'clock."

"And the wedding is still on?" I probably should've asked that first. I could see Mr. Rigatti retracting his blessing, and who could blame him? These two families obviously had issues.

"As far as I know."

"Okay, I'll be ready before then. And thank you again for breakfast. It looks perfect."

Michael kissed me on the top of my head. "Enjoy. I'll see you in a little bit."

After Michael left, I found my appetite once

more and dug into breakfast. I would've loved to make it a lazy morning, but I still needed to find a black dress for the wedding and get back to work. With the new connection between Mrs. Stein and the Rigattis, I wanted to go back to her apartment and see if I could dig up any other clues. Maybe the locked box held more than her will.

Less than an hour later, I was standing in front of Mrs. Stein's luxury condo complex. I walked with purpose, passing the doorman and marching over to the elevator, instructing the operator to take me to the top.

"Do you know if Miss Alice is at the Stein residence at the moment?" I asked the elevator operator as he closed the gold accordion gate before us.

"No, ma'am, she's not. But who might you be?"

"I am Valerie Reynolds, from the real estate company? Don't worry. I have a key." The elevator operator nodded as if that was good enough for him and let me off on the 10th floor.

Once off the elevator, I looked both ways down the hallway to make sure I was alone. Nothing but teal carpet and ivory wainscoting met my eye. I stood in front of the door and took a deep breath. Exhaling the air away, I placed my hand on the door handle and imagined inserting a key into the lock. With the pins in the proper alignment, the knob twisted freely in my hand.

The door swung open, and I smiled. The thrill of unlawful entry never got old. I crossed the threshold and started searching for clues. I didn't head straight to the bedroom. Instead, I walked around the common areas to see if anything jumped out at me. Landscapes, abstract, and expressionist paintings stared back at me. Based on the number of pieces of artwork still hanging on the wall, Alice hadn't gotten back to work after her nap. The poor woman. I couldn't imagine losing my best friend, Lexi. Even the thought of it kicked up my heart rate. My pulse thumped in my head. I took a deep breath to calm myself and refocus. I needed to look for clues.

I scanned the room once more, looking for anything that could connect Jill Stein to the Rigattis. For the hundredth time, I wondered why on earth Jill would leave so much money to them. Why would a witch care about shifter politics or have ties to the mafia? Did the paintings have something to do with it? Or could the coalition stand for something else that Jill was passionate about? At that point, I wasn't sure.

I opened kitchen drawers and rummaged through cabinets and magazine racks. Coming up empty, I stood in the kitchen for a moment and thought. Sandwiched on the counter between the kitchen sink and rotary telephone was the newspaper from earlier in the week. It was the Midnight Express, and Jill Stein was on the front page ... well, her lifeless body was. The top half of her was covered in a sheet, but her legs and bathrobe were exposed.

Nancy was right. It appeared Jill Stein dropped dead right in the middle of her foyer. Instinctively, I looked over at the exact spot where she was found. A shiver ran up my spine. I looked back at the photo and studied the details. Jill had either passed away sometime before going to bed or in the morning, given her attire. And what was that?

"Is that a saucer?" I held the picture up to my face, but it was too hard to tell. The image was cut out of the frame and out of focus. "Hm." I put the paper down and walked out of the kitchen and down the hall to Jill's bedroom.

In her room, I opened dresser drawers, checked the top of her closet and the bedside table, but didn't find anything noteworthy. I was about to walk over to the bed and pull the locked box out once more when I heard the front door open. Keys jingled as the visitor removed them from the lock and the door shut behind them. I ran and slid under the bed like a Major League Baseball player stealing home plate. I probably had the rug burn to prove it, too.

Alice was back, but she wasn't alone. I heard another woman's voice, but I couldn't clearly make it out. She stayed at the front of the apartment in the common rooms. It might have been Alice's daughter, as I thought I heard the woman say "mother" a time or two, but I wasn't sure. What I was certain of was that I was stuck under the bed while the women worked. I assumed they were taking down artwork and preparing the apartment for showing. At least that's what it sounded like.

An hour into the job, Alice walked into the bedroom. She was quiet, standing feet from the bed, her tan heels digging into the plush cream carpet. My heart pounded in my chest, waiting for her to make a move. I wondered what she wanted in the bedroom. Was she going to start clearing out Jill's personal possessions? I sure hoped not. I couldn't make myself disappear, but I could make Alice forget that she saw me. It would be trickier with two women in the house, though. Surely Alice would scream if she found me, and then I'd have to subdue Alice and whoever was with her and then erase their memories.

But I had to be ready to act if it came to that.

Alice stood, facing me. As quietly as possible, I scooted toward the other side of the bed, cognizant of the rolls of wrapping paper stored beside me, just waiting for me to crinkle them and give my location away.

After an eternity, which in reality was only a couple of minutes, Alice whispered, "I miss you, Jill," and then disappeared out of the room.

I sighed and closed my eyes. Disaster averted, for now.

TEN

The women finally left two hours after arriving. I waited a full five minutes after they were gone before rolling out from underneath the bed. Human instinct told me to get out of there quickly and take the stairs, but my magical instinct told me to slow down and take one more look. Over the years, I've learned to trust my magical intuition, which was why I took an extra minute to look around the room. That's when I spotted it.

Over on Jill's dresser, tucked behind her framed wedding portrait, was a smaller photograph, a colored one, which was still a rarity for the time, reserved for the wealthy like the Steins were. I took a closer look. The picture was of three women—Jill Stein, Alice Meyers, and Antonia Rigatti. The women wore formal summer wear with a beautiful cathedral as the backdrop. I had the feeling they were at a wedding, although whose, I couldn't say. The women held hands and smiled at the camera. It was clear from the photo they were friends or had been at one point. Another piece of the puzzle.

I left the picture as is and hightailed it out of there, taking the stairs down to the ground floor. I didn't need the elevator operator to ask any questions. I had spent much longer at the Steins' than I had intended. My free time was slipping away by the minute, but I still wanted to stop back at the hospital and check on Barbara Jean before looking for a dress. Hopefully, she was awake.

At the hospital, I bypassed the same less-than-friendly receptionist and took the stairs to the third floor.

I heard Barbara Jean's voice as I approached the room. "I can't believe I'm going to miss your wedding. This is so stupid."

"I know. I'm sorry, too," Mary replied.

"I wish I wasn't so tired. I swear, whoever did this to me is going to pay. That's a promise." It sounded like Barbara Jean yawned in the middle of the last sentence.

"Don't worry. The wedding's a disaster anyway. I

thought Papa was going to call the whole thing off last night."

"Do you think he still might?"

"Gosh, I hope not. I'm wild about Jim. But who knows how many guests will show up now."

"That bad?"

"Uh-huh. Uncle Micky even got in on the action."

"No way, isn't he like ninety?"

"Ninety-two, but that didn't stop him from running around the room, biting witches' ankles."

"He's always been a scrapper," Barbara Jean remarked.

"So true. That's why Papa loves him."

"Hey," I said, waving as I stood in the doorway and interrupted the conversation.

"Hey," Mary said. "Barbara Jean, do you remember Vee? She's Michael's girlfriend. We met her at the bakery yesterday."

"Vaguely. You look familiar, but that's about it." Barbara Jean shifted her weight to sit up more.

"How are you feeling?" I asked Barbara Jean.

"Like I'm going to rip the head off of the person who did this to me." Barbara Jean closed her eyes and sank back into the pillows. Her body seemed too weak to support herself for long. "As soon as I'm strong enough," she grumbled.

"Any idea what happened?" I asked.

"Not a clue. One minute I'm feeling fine, and the next, I'm at death's door. It hit me out of nowhere. If I were an average Joe, I'd be dead, I can tell you that."

"Or an average shifter," Mary said quietly.

"Benefit to being a grizzly, I guess. Fat lot it's doing me now, though. I have the energy of a sloth. Speaking of which, how's Ruthie?"

Mary rolled her eyes. "Being Ruthie. Sometimes I wish I could be more like her, though. Lost in my own world, slow to everything except to sleep. It's hard to get worked up about anything if you don't know what's going on." Mary sighed.

"She does have it pretty good, but I tell you one thing: It's a good thing she didn't get hit with this, you know? Because she wouldn't have gotten back up." Barbara Jean's comment caused Mary to burst into tears.

"Ah, shoot." Barbara Jean attempted to sit back up.

I rushed to Mary's side and wrapped my arm around her. She rested her head on my shoulder. "It'll be okay." I tried comforting her.

"I'm such an idiot. Don't listen to me." Barbara Jean tried to backtrack, but the damage was done. Mary's skin was red and blotchy like her tear-stained face. She quickly tried to use her fingers to wipe the tears away, but they were falling faster than she could erase them. Barbara Jean struggled to reach the box of tissues on the bedside table. Using my free arm, I stretched forward and got the box for her, plucking out two tissues and handing them to Mary.

"But you're right," Mary said, holding the tissues to her eyes. "If the attacker would've gone after Ruthie, we'd be planning her funeral." Again, more tears fell.

"Let's be thankful that it was me, then," Barbara Jean said. "I can handle it."

"It shouldn't have been anyone! I don't understand it. Who would do such a thing, and why?" Tears still ran down Mary's face despite her best efforts to stymie them.

"Don't worry, they'll figure it out." And by they, I meant me.

As much as Barbara Jean insisted that she wasn't tired, her energy was fading fast. The grizzly shifter could barely keep her eyes open. "It's fine, guys. Stay. You don't have to leave."

"Actually, I'm afraid we do. We have the rehearsal in a couple of hours, and I still need to find a dress," I said.

"Can I come with you?" Mary asked.

"I would love that. I need your opinion. You're the bride, after all." I tried cheering Mary up.

"You get some rest." Mary bent down to give Barbara Jean a hug. "I'll come back as soon as I can."

"I'm still going to kill whoever did this," Barbara Jean replied.

"Not if I get to them first," Mary said under her breath, but we all still heard her.

"I thought you didn't like conflict?" Barbara Jean asked, her eyes already closing.

"Not when it comes to my family. All bets are off." Mary looked off into the distance. I had a feeling she meant every word.

I'm not the type of girl who likes to shop. Shocking, I know. Mary, on the other hand, was. It's a good thing that we had a time limit, or Mary would have dragged me up one side and down the other of Michigan Avenue. Not that she still didn't give it a valiant effort. Who knew there were so many ankle-length black dresses? I was ready to pluck the first one off the rack and call it a day. But no, Mary insisted we try on every black dress that fit her criteria. Not only that, but even after I found one that I liked, she made the attendant put a hold on it until we could check out the other department stores.

"Remember, time crunch here," I said as Mary dragged me to the next high-end clothing store.

"You can't rush fashion. Besides, they can't start without me." Mary yanked open the store's door and marched past the doorman before he even knew we were there.

"Well, that's true, but still, we need to wrap this up soon," I said as I rushed to keep up with her stride.

When it was all said and done, I had tried on more black dresses in one day than I had in an entire lifetime before Mary declared one a winner.

"Would you like me to box this up?" the attendant asked.

"That would be great," I replied.

"No!" Mary exclaimed at the same time. "We need to have it steamed," Mary said to me. "Can you do that and have it delivered to The Duke?"

"It would be my pleasure," the woman replied automatically.

"The gloves and shoes too," Mary added.

"Of course," the woman smiled.

As Mary was the bride and her wedding weekend thus far had been a dumpster fire, I didn't argue.

"Shall I fetch you a cab, miss?" the department store doorman asked as we stepped outside.

"I'm okay with walking if you are." Mary turned to me.

Her comment caught me off guard. Weren't we in a hurry? Again, I didn't object. Mary obviously had something to say. "Walking is great."

Mary and I hooked a left and headed toward the hotel. I waited for her to speak. She wasted no time.

"You know, before this weekend, all I was worried about was the weather. Seems foolish now," Mary confessed.

"The weather is perfect," I admitted. You couldn't argue that. Sunny skies, the temperature in the mid-seventies—it was beautiful wedding weather.

"I always wanted an outdoor wedding, did you know that?" Mary didn't wait for me to answer. "Well, you didn't. But I always did. I was worried Papa wouldn't go for it since it's not traditional and all, but after Jim and I promised to have the wedding blessed in the church, he gave in. And now here I am, worrying the wedding won't even happen."

"Don't say that. Your wedding is going to happen, and it'll be beautiful."

"Well, I hope you're right. I know I'll breathe a sigh of relief after saying I do."

"I can understand that. I imagine this whole weekend has been stressful."

"To the hundredth degree." Mary thought for a moment. "But Jim's worth it. You know, I almost gave up on love before I met him."

"Why's that?" Not that I couldn't relate.

Mary shook her head. "I was always dating the

wrong guy. Men that worked for Papa or were only after one thing." Mary looked at me knowingly.

"Money?" I deadpanned.

Mary laughed. "Well, that too. The point is, I sure knew how to pick 'em."

"How did you meet Jim?"

"At that park of all places. A man had run off with my purse, and I cried for help. Too bad we can't shift in public, huh?"

"No doubt that would've given the thief pause."

"I know. But as it was, I yelled for help, and Jim came to my rescue."

"Talk about romantic."

"I know." Mary blushed. "It's been a whirlwind ever since." We walked on in silence for a minute before Mary said, "Maybe it's because I'm a shifter, I don't know, but the outdoors has always held a special place in my heart."

"I love being outdoors too. I actually live on a farm."

"You do?"

"Mm-hm. Well, I don't farm, but I live in the farmhouse."

"It must be so quiet out in the country."

"It can be, but I like it."

"So, how did you meet Michael? There's not a lot of farmland in New York City, is there?"

"Oh, um," I stammered. "I met him on vacation. We've been making the long-distance relationship work."

"Must have been some vacation."

"Believe me, it was." I smiled.

Mary sighed. "I hate to think someday all of this will be gone." She motioned to the open green space along Michigan Avenue. "They want to tear it all up and build parking lots and apartment buildings."

I winced. I'd hate for Mary to see what the downtown area looked like today. It would probably break her heart.

"Thankfully, though, I'm going to be able to save some of it," she added.

"You are?"

"You probably don't know her, but one of my mama's dear friends recently passed away, and I just found out that she left a large donation to the cause."

"Are you talking about Jill Stein?"

"You knew her?"

I almost stopped walking at the unexpected news. I thought up a story. "I just know Mrs. Stein recently passed and was a family friend."

"Mrs. Stein knew my plans to start purchasing property to establish parks. She helped me work on the nonprofit's mission statement and everything. It meant as much to her as it does to me. We were going to get started after the wedding. We had it all planned out." Mary shook her head in disbelief.

"You started a nonprofit?" I was trying to figure out where The Future is Tomorrow Coalition fit in.

"Well, Papa did, but he hadn't used it for years." I wondered if Mary knew the truth about her father. I wasn't going to bring it up, but then she added, "Well, nothing legal anyway." Mary shook her head as if she didn't approve. "Now I can change that." Mary set her shoulders straight. "I'm so grateful to Mrs. Stein. She was a wonderful woman."

"She sounds like it." Now I knew why the heiress changed her will. It had nothing to do with the mafia but with her desire to create a legacy. That made sense and seemed to align with her values; well, what I knew of them anyway.

"Mrs. Stein was going to be on the Board of Directors, but the best I can do now is have a park named in her honor."

"She would've liked that." Even though I had never met the woman, I had a feeling that it would have meant something to her.

"I think so," Mary replied thoughtfully. "Mrs. Stein was a champion of noble causes, conservation being just one on her list. I can't believe she's gone. None of us can. Especially Mama."

Mary continued to talk about her plans for the

nonprofit the entire walk back to the hotel. If she had her way, she would secure enough green space for future Chicagoans for years to come. Now that I thought of it, present-day Chicago had plenty of parks. Perhaps Mary's plans came to fruition after all.

ELEVEN

Given the recent turn of events, I would have loved nothing more than to draw up a hot bath and think the case through, but maid of honor duties called, and we were already running dangerously close to being late. I dashed into my hotel room as Michael was straightening his tie. I kicked off my shoes and began to undress while filling him in.

"Sorry, I met up with Mary, and we went shopping. Let me tell you, that woman can shop. Whew. But, we found a dress for tomorrow, so yay."

Michael looked behind me as if expecting to see a dress.

"It's being delivered later today." I selected another dress from Michael's collection and slipped it over my head. "Zip me, please?" Michael obliged, and I dashed into the bathroom to freshen my hair and makeup. We were ready to roll out in ten minutes flat, which was impressive even by my standards.

"What are those for?" Michael asked as I yanked out half the tissue box and stuffed them in my purse.

"Just trust me on this one."

Michael shrugged and left it at that.

The Bay Shore Country Club was about a twenty-minute car ride north of downtown. Mr. Rigatti had arranged for a car service to take the wedding party to the club. I sat with Michael in the backseat of the Lincoln Continental while the driver navigated us out of downtown traffic and into the more suburban, upscale neighborhood of Water Creek.

I was lost in my thoughts, wondering where to look for clues next. With an explanation for Mrs. Stein's will, the Rigattis were no longer suspects. I had to expand my list and dig further into the victims' backgrounds. Easier said than done when it came to the likes of Xavier James. The vampire hunter was in the wind, as we liked to say in this business. He was going from town to town, job to job, and leaving no trace of his existence. Up until recently, I had been the same, always requesting a fake identity from the Agency and never revealing my true self while working a case. Michael changed all that.

"What are you thinking about?" Michael asked.

"Hm?" I had been looking out the window at the passing scenery when I turned to Michael. "What's that?"

"What's on your mind?"

I remembered my promise to help Michael relax and enjoy the weekend before I replied. "I was thinking about how great it would be to come back here when we're not rushed with a wedding. It'd be nice to relax for a few days, wouldn't it?"

"It would. Maybe in the summertime?"

"Oh, most definitely." Midwest winters in Michigan were brutal enough. I had no desire to throw in the crazy wind chills Chicago was famous for.

"And take in a Cubs game," Michael added.

"Now, you're talking. Just leave the hotdog off the table." I held my hand up in a stopping motion.

Michael laughed. "Thank you for doing this."

I cocked my head. "Doing what exactly?"

"This," Michael said, motioning to my dress and the country club coming into view. "You didn't have to be the maid of honor and let Mary drag you all over."

"You should've seen all the dresses," I jokingly lamented and then added in a more serious tone, "I just did what anyone would do."

"Not true. Most women would complain about not having enough notice, or they don't like the wedding colors or the style of dress the bride picked out. Believe me, I've stood up in my fair share of weddings. I know how it could've gone down."

I laughed because that was true. Women were known to get a little crazy when it came to weddings, even when they weren't their own.

"You're right. How about I just say you're welcome then?"

"Thank you for being you." Michael leaned over and gave me a quick kiss.

I didn't know what to say to that. A moment later, the driver put the car in park, and the valet opened my door. I hoped Michael would say the same thing if he knew I was working a case. I tried not to let the guilt eat away at me from being so secretive by reminding myself why I was doing it.

"Wow, this is nice," I remarked as I stepped outside the car. In front of us stood a sprawling stone ranch. The outside comprised dinner-plate-sized river stones that I was betting were natural rocks instead of the facade people plastered onto the front of houses nowadays.

Rolling hills and dunes dotted the property, contrasting with the manicured lawn of the club's golf course.

We walked up the stone steps, through the double doors of the country club, and into the generous great room. The club's leather chairs and warm woods invited guests to sit back, relax, and visit for a bit. An enormous fireplace hearth rose along the south wall matching the stonework out front, adding to the grandness.

I turned to the back of the clubhouse and looked out the wall of windows onto the large outdoor patio.

"This way." Michael took my hand, and together we walked through the sliding glass door and onto the gray-slate patio, where an acre pond with an impressive fountain stood as the focal point, the pump spraying water high into the air. The country club had a white pergola across the front of the patio for the bride and groom to stand in front of. Hanging baskets overflowed with yellow and white begonias, and potted arborvitaes set off an aisle. The staff had already set out rows of white chairs on each side for tomorrow's guests.

"This is beautiful," I said to no one in particular.

It was Mary that replied. "It's perfect, isn't it?" she said, teary-eyed. I tugged one of the tissues free from my purse and handed it over.

Michael smirked. "Always prepared," he said out of the corner of his mouth.

"I had a feeling," I replied softly.

"Oh, thank you," Mary said, accepting the tissue. "I promise I'll get it all out of my system today."

I doubted that, and that was perfectly okay.

Mary looked around the patio. "Mama, where's Papa?"

"He had some business to attend to, but don't worry. He'll join us for dinner," Antonia Rigatti replied. Mary's mother looked regal. She wore a deep purple dress with a coordinating jacket embellished with gold thread. The material reflected the sunlight and highlighted the green in her eyes. If a lion was the king of the jungle, a lioness wasn't far behind.

Jim's mother, Sally, was a study in opposites, having worn black slacks and a white blouse. Her hair was still untamed, and if you didn't know her name, you'd mistake her for waitstaff. Well, except for the bangles. She wore a stack of them on her wrists. I watched her casually reach her hand into her pocket and pull out a small white pill. She turned and swallowed it down without any water.

"Mom, what do you think?" Jim called over his shoulder.

"What?" She was visibly startled.

"For the ceremony. Isn't this great?" Jim replied, taking Mary's hand in his.

"Sure," Sally replied on the exhale, her eyes darting around the property.

I tried to keep my brow from furrowing, but it was harder to do than one might think.

"I know that look," Michael replied, looking down at me. "What's wrong."

I cleared my throat. "Nothing. I just remembered some paperwork I left unfinished back home. But it can wait."

"Staring at all of this," Michael gestured to the lovely landscaping, "made you think of work?"

"No, staring at my handsome boyfriend made me think of work," I improvised.

"Well, you're forgiven then."

"Why, thank you."

I looked beyond the patio at the rest of the property. A well-maintained barn was to the far right where the manicured lawn ended, and woods and riding trails took over. On the other side of the property was the archery range that butted up against the golf clubhouse. The overhang of the range was designed in the same style as the main clubhouse but smaller. I could barely make out the details. I assumed that the property layout was designed to keep the majority of the recreational activities out of sight of the main clubhouse and its pristine nature views. But, I'd bet if we walked around long enough, we'd stumble upon tennis courts and horseshoe pits, just like I was willing to wager the main building housed an indoor swimming pool and at least a few bowling lanes.

"Shall we get started?" Jim asked, looking around for the priest. Spotting him, Jim motioned for the priest to begin.

"This is so exciting!" Mary sniffled as tears of happiness glinted in her eyes.

After practicing how we'd walk in and where we'd stand, the priest walked us through the ceremony.

"Now, this is the part where the two of you will exchange vows," the white-collared clergymen instructed Jim and Mary.

"Our vows." Mary cried as she repeated the phrase. "Oh my goodness, I can't believe this is really happening."

Jim and Mary were facing one another. Jim lovingly squeezed Mary's hands. "Are you going to be okay?" he asked.

"Yes, I'm just so excited."

"I am too," Jim replied, gazing into Mary's eyes.

"I can't believe it's tomorrow." Mary sighed in contentment.

The two lovebirds shared a moment. I glanced at the parents in attendance, sitting in the white, H-backed chairs on their respective sides. Antonia rolled her eyes and sighed in exasperation while

Sally cast her eyes down as she silently shook her head. Luckily neither Jim nor Mary caught their looks.

Thankfully, the rehearsal was almost finished. It was a good thing, too, as I was out of tissues. A few minutes later, the staff escorted us to a private room off the main dining area. Unlike the main dining room, which was decorated in shades of blue—a soft tone on the walls and a darker shade for the drapes and chairs—this room was decorated in shades of yellow. I doubted that was by coincidence, as the room housed the faint smell of fresh paint fumes. Bouquets of white calla lilies were placed every few feet or so down the long table, which was set up to seat twelve. There were only ten of us since Frank and Dotty had left. Jim's parents reluctantly sat across from Mary's parents, but not before Sally looked longingly over at the two empty chairs at the end of the table. But when Jim sat next to her, she was forced to stay put.

"This room is perfect!" Mary exclaimed as she sat down. "I just love yellow." She smiled broadly at Jim.

If I had been hoping for some cheese ravioli or thick garlic bread, I'd be sorely disappointed. Instead, platter after platter of smoked, grilled, roasted, and basted meat came from the kitchen following the appetizer and salad courses. Mr. Rigatti beamed with pride. I plastered a smile on my face so as not to offend the apex predator and looked forward to the dessert course. Ruthie's date, Adam (which, if you asked me, was far too normal of a name for the aardvark), was seated next to me.

"You like jazz?" he asked, snapping his fingers and bee bopping in his chair.

I nodded. "Sure. I like it enough."

"That's cool, man. Real cool." Adam closed his eyes and swayed to the music in his head.

Michael smirked from across the table. I turned to engage Jim, sitting on the other side of me, but the groom was too busy trying to facilitate conversation between his parents and the Rigattis. "The Rigattis have a vacation home in Florida, and you enjoy visiting the Sunshine State," he said between the two groups.

"Isn't he dreamy?" Ruthie said to Michael while gazing at Adam.

"You've landed quite a catch there," Michael replied with a straight face. I lowered my eyes and shook my head to keep myself from laughing.

The rest of the dinner passed in much the same fashion, with Michael and me sandwiched between the bride and groom and the odd couple, which gave us plenty of time to observe the guests, a favorite pastime for detectives, working a case or not.

"And do you sell these ... creations?" Antonia asked Sally after she brought up her love of quilting.

"Oh, no. I usually donate them or give them as gifts." Sally looked down at her fingers while she spoke.

"Charming." Antonia looked at her daughter with an expression that suggested she'd rather be caught dead than give a quilt as a gift. For her part, Mary smiled kindly at Sally, even though her future mother-in-law was still fidgeting and looking down.

At the end of the table, the fathers seemed to be getting along just fine. Stan, eating forkful after forkful of pork tenderloin, kept Vito entertained, recounting his craziest customers at the car dealership he owns.

"Let me ask you something. Square footage wise, which car has the biggest trunk?" Vito asked Stan. I almost dropped my fork and wanted to tell Stan not to answer that question. Nothing good could come out of a mafia boss asking that question.

"Oh well, I'd have to think about that for a moment." Stan looked up at the ceiling and seemed to calculate a few variables.

"Rough estimate?" Vito asked.

I looked to Michael, and he, too, seemed genuinely interested in the question.

I never did hear the answer as Jim's compliment caught my attention.

"Mom's an excellent cook," he looked proudly at his mom. Sally scoffed but looked pleased nonetheless at her son's compliment.

"I bet she is," Antonia replied, looking down her nose. "Tell me, do you speak French?"

Sally turned her attention to Antonia, seeming confused at the change in topic. "Excuse me?"

"Do you speak French?" Antonia spoke slowly as if Sally were stupid.

"Oh ... no, sorry," Sally replied.

"Italian?" Antonia tried again.

Sally shook her head and pulled back from the conversation.

"I speak at least three languages, as does Mary. I believe competency in a romantic language is a sign of a well-rounded woman." Antonia nodded to her daughter, who was seated next to her. I was about to jump in the conversation and say that I only spoke one as well, unless you counted hand gestures, when Mary said, "But Sally's a master of the English language. Jim's told me all about the stories you've written." Mary's compliment was genuine.

Sally blushed.

"You must let me read them then," Antonia insisted.

"Oh no, they're really not for adults." Sally shook her head.

"But if Mary's read them," Antonia let her voice trail off.

"Maybe someday then." Sally looked to her son to change the topic of conversation, but Antonia wouldn't drop it.

"Are they published?" she asked.

"Only by me," Sally quipped.

"Well, then. Perhaps you can lend me a copy. I'm quite a fan of literature."

"Well, these definitely aren't for you then. There's nothing literary about them. They're more like nursery rhymes, fables. You know, morals and the like. Clearly, something you're not interested in," Sally finished with a smile. My mouth almost hit the table at Sally's retort, and then I smiled and thought, *Good for you*, and hoped that would shut Antonia's mouth for a minute or two.

Antonia cleared her throat and replied, "Well, nevertheless," but didn't finish her thought.

After dinner, some of the guests had already started to disperse while others were still finishing their mignardises and coffee. Ruthie was one of them, but now that I knew she was a sloth shifter, it didn't surprise me. Her date did earn a side-eye from me when he bent low and sniffed his cloth napkin. I thought that weird enough until he cautiously tasted it. Shaking his head, he dropped the napkin and let his nose guide him forward to inspect the flowers. I looked away, not wanting to see what he did next. Dinner had been fraught with tension. I couldn't handle much more. Not without opening my mouth, and that never ended well. I decided I needed a break.

"I'll be right back," I said to Michael, excusing myself to use the restroom. I left the private dining area and was rounding the corner when I stopped short.

Standing in the hallway opposite the coat check-in, in the enclave between the bathrooms, was Jim and his mother, Sally.

"I just don't want you to make a mistake." Sally's voice was pleading.

"Mom, don't worry."

"How can I not worry? I'm your mother. And you barely know this girl. Why are you in such a hurry to marry her?"

"It's not that we're in a rush—"

"But you are, and I don't understand it."

"I wish you'd relax."

"I can't help it. This whole wedding business makes me very nervous."

Jim put both of his hands on his mom's shoulders

and spoke calmly to her. "I love her, Mom. That's it. And I know you love me, which is why I need you to support me. Mary's a sweet girl. I promise. "

"If you say so. Her parents—"

Now it was Jim's turn to interrupt. "Mary is nothing like her parents. Believe me, you'll like her. Give her a chance."

Sally sighed. "I don't want you making a mistake like your brother."

My ears pricked up. Jim has a brother? How didn't I know this, and where the heck is he?

"I'm not Carl, Mom."

I thought briefly back to the other night when Michael asked where Carl was, and Frank replied that he was drunk.

"I know, but I would've never expected him to change the way he has. Your wife can influence you in ways you'd never imagine."

"Mary's not like that. She's not trying to change me or control me."

"Not yet, but she might, and you'll be a different person like your brother. You'll end up like them." Sally used her knuckle to wipe a lone tear from under her eye and sniffed. "He can't even put the bottle down long enough to come tonight."

Jim closed his eyes and took a calming breath. "I promise I won't change."

"That's not something you can promise." Sally patted her son's hand. "Especially with a father-in-law like that."

Jim was left speechless. Probably because he knew his mother was right.

I cleared my throat and started walking with purpose toward the bathroom to give mother and son ample notice of my presence. Sally stepped aside, and I smiled at the duo, her eyes threatening to spill more tears as I walked into the restroom. As I stood in front of the mirror, washing my hands, I took a second to consider Sally. She hadn't been a suspect, but maybe she should be.

"What if it wasn't a curse?" I asked my reflection. "What if it was poison, and Mary was the intended target?"

If Sally wanted to stop the wedding from taking place, maybe delay it a bit to talk some sense into her son, then poisoning the bride would be one way to do it. Michael had said Sally was an expert potions master. Poisoning and potions went hand in hand. But what about the other attacks? Could Sally have a tie-in with them also? I didn't know of any off the top of my head, but it wasn't too far of a stretch to think Jill Stein and Sally might have been friends. They were, after all, witches living in the same community.

As for Bernie and Xavier, all it might require is digging into Sally's background a bit more.

I shook the water off my hands and dried them on a paper towel before exiting the restroom. When I did, neither Jim nor his mother was standing outside anymore, but Michael was.

"Ready to go?" he asked.

"I thought you would never ask."

TWELVE

"You know, most brides like to call it an early night the day before the wedding," I said as the driver dropped us off in front of the jazz club. Green neon outlined the perimeter of the club's sign, which advertised live entertainment and one-dollar gimlets. Maybe I was still in detective mode and not feeling the club scene, or I'd become cheap drinking thirty-five-cent glasses of wine, but a dollar for a mixed drink didn't seem like that much of a deal.

"I'll have to keep that in mind," Michael said as he held his hand out for me to take. His response left me shocked. What was that supposed to mean?

"Keep what in mind?" I stood frozen, looking up at Michael standing on the curb, hand extended, waiting for me to take it. Surely, he wasn't referring to our future wedding. He wouldn't be that presumptuous now, would he? Or was it even being presumptuous at this point? We had been dating for six months—okay, more like eight now that I thought about it—and with Michael being a mid-century man, well, I assumed he only expected me to be thinking of marriage.

"Oh, honey, the look on your face. It's cute, really. Terrified but cute."

"I do not have a look on my face." I stepped out of the car, bypassing Michael's hand.

"Your fear of commitment is only one of the many things I love about you," Michael said behind me.

I scoffed and walked toward the entrance, tugging harder on the door than I meant to, which only looked more ridiculous when Jim attempted to open it for me from the inside. The result was the groom tumbling back out the door.

"Oh, my goodness. I'm sorry, I didn't even see you there," I said, a bit embarrassed.

Jim caught his balance after tripping onto the sidewalk. "Your girl's got some grip, Mike."

"That she does." Michael clapped Jim on the shoulder, and I held the door open for the two of them, rolling my eyes at Michael as he passed, and trailed in after.

After that little incident, I vowed to put my detective hat away and enjoy the night.

The lighting inside was dim, with domed candles in the center of the tables casting light on patrons' faces and the checkered black-and-white floor. Booths lined the perimeter, and low, black-lacquered tables seating two to four patrons crowded the floor, not leaving much space in front of the stage.

A long bar stood opposite the stage. Large, square, mirrored tiles reflected the bartenders' backs, highlighting their ungodly speed as they mixed and poured drinks. The bartenders were as much of a sight to me as the entertainment with the way their porcelain skin glowed in the darkness. Their skin reflected just enough light to make out the details, like how their hair was tied behind their backs in low ponytails and their slightly elongated canines when they smiled. The men moved so fast that their hands blurred. And yet none of the patrons seemed to notice. They were too enamored with the performer on stage.

The moment the singer sang that first note, I snapped my head up and saw Edith Adams commanding center stage. It took me a second to remember how to walk. Edith was that good. I could get lost in her voice for hours.

A section of high-top tables had been pushed

together and reserved for us in the back corner, closer to the bar. I found my feet and followed the group, taking a seat next to Michael. Drinks were ordered, and we all took a minute to watch Edith wrap up her set. The moment the last note rang out, the crowd hooted and hollered appreciatively, and then the party really got started. Tunes flowed out of the jukebox, and chatter mixed with laughter picked up. Purple mood lighting replaced the center stage spotlight, and staff worked to clear the now-empty tables in front of the stage, creating a dance floor.

"Where did these come from?" I asked the group as a shot glass had magically appeared before me.

"Don't look at me," Jim replied, nodding his head toward Michael, who was finishing passing the shot glasses out to everyone, including Ruthie and Adam, who had finally arrived. Michael picked up his glass, and the rest of us followed suit.

"Now that we're all here, it's time to properly celebrate the future Mr. and Mrs. Wilson. To the best couple this city has ever seen. Can't wait for the real party tomorrow, but until then, to Mary and Jim!" Michael held his shot up. We all replied, "To Mary and Jim," and downed our drinks.

Oh, that burns, I thought to myself before saying to Michael, "Tequila, really?" I frantically looked around for a lemon slice but came up empty. My brow furrowed, and I coughed.

"What? It was good," Michael's nostrils flared, probably from the burn.

"Mary will never forgive you if we're all hungover tomorrow." I had been serious, but when I looked over at Mary, her eyes were bright and wild, and she seemed to be having the time of her life. "I stand corrected."

"Ha!" Michael laughed before pulling me close to him and kissing me on the top of my head.

"Xavier?" Jim's voice rose above the crowd. "Is that you, man? No way. You're in town?" Jim came around the tables and shook the vampire hunter's hand. For his part, Xavier reached in for a one-armed hug.

"I heard the good news. Good for you." Xavier caught my eye. Recognition crossed his face for a split second before he wiped the expression away. Outwardly, I smiled in response, while internally, I tried to put another piece of the puzzle together. Jim knew Xavier. What did that mean?

"Xavier, meet my bride-to-be, Mary." Jim beamed with pride.

"Nice to meet you," Mary replied, shaking Xavier's hand. I would have bought her response if she hadn't started fidgeting with her necklace and a red rash hadn't suddenly appeared on her neck. I'd bet any amount of money that Xavier was no stranger to her.

"Join us for a drink?" Jim asked Xavier. Michael was already signaling to the waitress to bring another round.

"Yeah, man. I can stay for one." Xavier pulled over a barstool from the main bar and straddled it.

Mary's eyes darted around the room. You didn't need to be an empath to tell how uncomfortable she was. I couldn't even catch her eye.

"Dance with me?" Adam asked Ruthie, his eyes full of excitement. He was totally in his element. It took a second for Ruthie to accept, and Adam dragged her onto the dance floor. Not because Ruthie wasn't agreeable, but rather, she wasn't moving fast enough for Adam's dancing feet. Adam snapped his fingers and be-bopped along to the music, swinging his hands and singing along. He appeared to be dancing the jive; either that, or he had a tick from the way his head kept twitching. Ruthie copied Adam, making the same moves, except it was as if she was submerged in wet cement, moving in slow motion.

After a couple of minutes of watching the couple dance, Mary announced that she would be back and stood abruptly, leaving the party of five. Xavier watched Mary walk away while pretending to listen to Jim. Minutes later, Xavier excused himself as well. For my part, I tried to engage in conversation, but I was really more interested in the dynamics at play at the table, and when Xavier left, I gave up trying.

"I'm going to go use the restroom. I'll be right back," I told Michael, leaving before he could ask me anything. Thankfully, Michael didn't notice anything afoot as he and Jim went back to talking about the good old days.

I found Xavier and Mary talking at the end of the hallway, past the bathrooms, near the emergency exit. Back here, the lighting was even darker. The exit sign above the door cast their features in an eerie red light. Their details were hard to make out, but I could clearly hear their voices.

"I thought you wanted to change the world. Make a difference." Xavier sounded incredulous. I could picture him shaking his head in disbelief.

"I am making a difference!" The defiance in Mary's voice was strong.

"How? By planting flowers and painting park benches? You're a strong, talented shifter."

"I know what I am."

"Then, why? Why throw it all away? Jell-O molds and meatloaf? That isn't you."

"What's your point?"

"You're not a housewife. You deserve more," Xavier continued.

"Oh, and you were going to give me that?"

"You know I was."

"The only thing you left me with was a broken heart."

"I told you I'd be back."

"Ha," Mary scoffed. "You had your chance. You chose to leave. I warned you I wasn't going to wait."

"But now I'm back. I came home for you. It's not too late. Come with me. We can leave right now. Walk out that door and never look back. Think of it, you and me together? Those rogue vamps won't stand a chance."

Mary hesitated. "Xavier—"

"Come on, Mary, you know you're destined for greatness."

Mary sighed and shook her head. "Promises. You're great at making them."

"And keeping them."

"No. Not keeping them. You only get to fool me once."

Xavier threw his arms up in frustration. "How can I prove myself to you?"

"You don't get to. We're done."

"Don't say that. Just give me time. Please, whatever you do, just don't marry Jim."

"Jim is more of a man than you'll ever be."

"Jim is a tool. I've known him my whole life. He's an idiot."

SMACK. Mary's hand moved in a flash. It was already resting at her side before Xavier moved to block her. A set of four claw marks raked across his cheek, the blood trail making them visible. My breath caught.

"I don't ever want to see you again. Stay away from us." Mary's voice was cold and calculating. A shiver ran up my spine. Where was the teary-eyed bride of earlier? She certainly wasn't here.

I turned to hurry away from the duo before they saw me standing there and walked right into Edith. "Oh, I'm sorry. Excuse me." I planned to step aside from the singer and hightail it back to our table, but Edith stopped me.

"Hey! How's it going? You're the girl from the basement, right?" Edith's brow was damp, but her grin was wide with that fresh off a performance high.

"Yeah, that was me." And the wedding meet and greet disaster, I thought. Which reminded me, seeing Edith was at the wedding party when all heck broke loose, chances were she was a supernatural of some sort. Either that or her and the band's memory had been erased. "You were great tonight. Really," I added, keeping the conversation going.

"Oh, thanks so much. The Green Light is my favorite club to perform at."

"Well, it shows. Buy you a drink?"

"Sure, my set's done for the night."

We walked over to the bar, and despite there being a line, the bartender looked past the other patrons and made eyes with Edith.

"Gin martini. Straight up." She then turned to me.

"Same," I hollered back. In the background, Bobby Darin's Dream Lover on the jukebox competed with the ambient noise.

"So, are you from Chicago?" I asked Edith.

"Born and raised. What about you?"

"Well, I'm a Midwestern girl, too. Only a bit further east. Michigan."

"Ah, on the other side of the lake then."

"You got it."

"Been that way a time or two. A lot of corn."

"And cows," I joked, which was true, especially in mid-century Michigan.

Edith and I continued to chat, and I tried to keep my eye out for when Xavier and Mary re-joined the table, but Xavier never returned. He must've walked straight out the back exit, not that I blamed him. How would he explain the scratches across his cheek without drawing a scene? Mary, on the other hand, did return, and she looked cool and calm as can be. That only raised my suspicion of her and made me rethink the Rigattis' involvement in Jill Stein's murder. Could Mary have been the one to pull the metaphorical trigger? Ten million dollars was a lot of cash, and what if Mary knew Jill had changed her will and was giving her nonprofit the bulk of her fortune? That type of money was a strong motive for murder.

I was doing a good job of keeping my eye on Mary until Michael decided to join Edith and me. Then a couple of Edith's bandmates joined us, and we started to have our own side party. The band had been on tour the past three months, and the stories they could tell were making us all laugh.

"Remember that time Martin got locked out of the motel in only his underwear?" Ralph, the bass player, asked.

"Where did he think he put the key?" Edith replied.

Martin blushed and shook his head. "Nah, nah, don't listen to them. I had a shirt on too," he deadpanned. More laughter ensued.

"Hey, buddy, sorry to leave you over there," Michael said to Jim when he joined our group. "I thought you and Mary might want a little bit of downtime together."

"Yeah, we did. Thanks for that," Jim replied.

I looked over Jim's shoulder. "Where is Mary?"

"Oh, she said the noise was giving her a bit of a headache, and she wanted to be her best for tomorrow," Jim said matter-of-factly.

"So she left?" I asked.

"I put her in the cab myself," Jim stated with a head nod.

"Oh." I couldn't hide the alarm in my voice.

"I know, I know. I should've gone with her, but she wouldn't hear of it. Bad luck to see the bride before the wedding day and all," Jim tapped his watch, misreading my comment. I wasn't worried about Mary heading to the hotel by herself or tomorrow but rather wondered if that's really where she was headed.

"You know, I should probably get going too," I said. I finished the last of my martini and looked over at Michael. He was talking to Martin in earnest after finding out they're both native New Yorkers. I knew he wasn't ready to call it a night, which was perfectly all right with me. It would give me a chance to check in on Mary without any questions asked.

"You heading out?" Edith asked me when I stood.

"Yeah. Big day tomorrow," I replied.

"I'll walk with you," she said.

"Oh, sure." I had planned on taking a cab, but it

wasn't every day that Edith Adams asked you to walk her home.

Michael caught my hand and tugged me back to him. I leaned down. "Are you sure you don't want me to come with you?" he asked.

"I'm fine. Promise. You have fun." I kissed Michael on his cheek. "See you in a little bit."

We said our goodbyes and left the Green Light.

"I like to walk for a bit after our shows," Edith explained as we stepped outside. City traffic cruised on by, the bright automobiles of yesterday that I had fallen in love with, the colorful city lights and neon reflecting off their polished hoods. "It helps me burn off the leftover energy," Edith continued. "You live in the neighborhood, right?"

"Actually, no."

"You don't? Oh, man, I'm sorry. I shouldn't have assumed. Are you even headed my way?"

"Yeah, I'm staying at The Duke."

"You don't even live here? Now I'm really sorry."

"Don't be. It's fine. Promise."

We walked for a few minutes in relative silence. It was a bright, warm night, the kind that brought people out to enjoy the weather. In my opinion, there wasn't anything like a nice summer night in the Midwest. Okay, so technically it wasn't summer for a couple more weeks, but Mother Nature hadn't gotten that memo. The weather was comfortable, and the breeze felt nice.

"So, did you find out anything else about crabby Mr. Compton?" Edith asked.

"Not much, to be honest. I'm still working on wrapping my head around the suspects and the motives, and the victims."

"The 'Scared to Death' cases," Edith remarked.

"Exactly. I have multiple victims, multiple suspects, and the clock is against me."

"You're not staying here long?"

"In Chicago? No. I'm only here for a wedding."

"You know, I played a gig at The Duke this week. Just a couple of days ago. It was real wild," Edith said.

The fact that Edith remembered the gig added weight to my suspicion that she was a supernatural, although she didn't give off the scent of a shifter, and I wasn't picking up a vampire vibe either. Seeing as the woman clearly wasn't an apparition or an animated corpse most likely meant she was a witch.

"I know. I saw you there," I confessed.

"You did?" Edith swatted at my hand as if she couldn't believe it.

"That's the wedding that I'm talking about. I came in town for the Wilson and Rigatti wedding when a case fell into my lap."

"Girl, you should've said something. Wasn't that

crazy? Whose side were you on, the bride's or the groom's?"

"Technically, the groom's, but I wasn't taking sides. More like trying to keep the peace."

"That's brave of you. Tell you what, it was the Rigattis that hired me, but once those teeth and claws came out, I hightailed it out of there. My talents are of the witchy variety, but all my magic went to my voice. I couldn't curse a fly, let alone a lion."

"Yeah, it was nuts for sure."

"You know, I thought they were going to cancel that wedding, but I'm still scheduled for tomorrow."

"They hired you for the wedding too?"

"Mr. Rigatti's a big fan. I'm singing at the ceremony, and the band and I are the reception's entertainment. It's the least I could do. Mr. Rigatti's the one that got me into all the clubs downtown here. From there, it's been one thing after another, like going on tour. I really am grateful even if he has a bit of a temper."

"Temper?" I figured the man had to have some aggression being who he was and what he did for a living, but I hadn't heard anyone discuss it directly.

"Woo-wee! You don't want to be on that man's bad side. Best to keep the boss man happy. And that's exactly what I intend to do."

"So, you'll be there tomorrow?"

"Absolutely. Although I might ask my mama for a protection spell or something beforehand. Just in case."

"Yeah, just in case."

CRACK!

The bullet dug into the brick building behind us, hitting the corner. Red dust and chunks of hardened cement fell onto the sidewalk.

"Get down," I yelled, yanking Edith by her wrist as we dove to the ground. My knees dug into the cement sidewalk as we army crawled, seeking cover under a nearby parked car.

"Ping! Ping!" The bullets tore into the car's metal exterior. The gun wasn't loud. It must've been cloaked with magic, but that didn't mean the bullets wouldn't hurt.

"Who in the world is shooting at us?" Edith asked, panic filling her voice.

I didn't answer. I was too busy trying to see where the shots were coming from. There was an alleyway kitty-corner, and I was almost certain that's where the shooter was. I couldn't see anywhere else that offered cover.

It was dark, but the city wasn't asleep. Cabs whizzed by, and up ahead, people were walking completely unaware. We waited a bit to see if the shooter would strike again, but it was silent. I debated what to do. My fighting instinct told me to run into the alley and see if I could catch up with the attacker, but what if that's what they expected me to do and they were waiting in ambush? I was a lone ranger here, and without backup, that wasn't a smart thing to do.

Edith and I sat with our backs against the car as I thought my next steps through.

"They were shooting at you, weren't they?" Edith asked me. "Tell me they were shooting at you."

"Probably," I said, resting my head against the car door before rolling my head to the side to look at Edith. "You okay?"

"Yeah, better than you. Your knees are all scraped up." Edith motioned to my kneecaps, where sure enough, I was bleeding.

"Well, at least there are no bullet holes," I said.

"Does this mean you're closer to solving your case?"

"What do you mean?"

"Well, obviously somebody thinks you're onto something, or they wouldn't be shooting at you."

I sighed and closed my eyes. "Good point."

We sat there for a few more seconds in silence before cautiously standing up. Other people, after all, were walking the streets, and a group was even approaching the front of the alleyway where I believed the shots were fired from. I figured the shooter wouldn't be crazy enough to shoot through them to try to hit me.

Edith and I made a break for it as soon as the group passed in front of the alleyway entrance, and Edith hailed the first cab she saw.

"How about we ride the rest of the way?" she said, ducking inside.

"You read my mind."

At this point, Edith's apartment building was not more than two blocks away, and the cab driver looked at us like we were a little goofy when Edith asked him to pull over and let her out, probably wondering why we hadn't just walked. Neither one of us felt like explaining.

"See you tomorrow. Be careful, okay?" she said when she got out.

"Yeah, you too," I replied before she shut the door. I had the cab drop me off at The Duke, paid the driver a dollar, which was a pretty nice tip, and headed inside the supernatural digs. Part of me wanted to get washed up and get my knee taken care of as soon as possible, but the other part wanted to see if Mary was in her hotel suite. Detective work won out, and I bypassed my hotel room and marched straight to hers, or maybe it was more like a limp, seeing as my knees were starting to hurt something fierce.

I knocked on Mary and Ruthie's suite door three times.

"Hey, Mary, it's Vee. Are you in there?" I waited a bit but didn't hear anything. I knocked again and waited, but still nothing. I knew where Ruthie was. The question was, where was Mary? I had to play it smart. I didn't want to risk breaking in and bumping into her coming out of the shower and then having to scramble her memory.

"Hmm," I thought out loud. I ended up retracing my steps and going back down to the hotel front desk. "Excuse me," I asked the clerk, a shifter, I believe. "Did you see Mary Rigatti come through here a little bit ago?"

"I'm sorry, ma'am, I haven't, but my shift just started at the top of the hour. Would you like me to ring her for you?" The clerk looked behind his shoulder at the clock. It was just after ten o'clock.

"If you don't mind, it's important." While the clerk dialed Mary's room, I tried to think of an excuse as to why I would be calling at this time of night. I didn't want Mary to know that someone had shot at Edith and me.

But I ended up not needing an excuse because Mary didn't answer.

"Would you like me to leave a message for when she does come in?" the clerk asked.

"No, that's okay. I'll catch up with her later." I thanked the clerk and walked back to Mary's room.

Taking a calming breath, I put my hand on the lock and felt the bolt magically slide back. The knob twisted freely in my hand, and I opened the door.

"Mary, hello? Are you here?" The room was dark and quiet. Cautiously, I walked in and surveyed the space. The suite was laid out with two queen beds, a desk, a small table, and two lounge chairs. The bathroom was right off the entrance. Mary's and Ruthie's personal belongings were set up on the dressers, and I imagined the twin closets were full of their clothes. I didn't stay long, just a quick visit to make sure Mary wasn't there. I headed for my hotel room after that to get cleaned up and try to figure out what I was missing.

THIRTEEN

I fell asleep sometime after eleven o'clock and didn't even wake up when Michael came in. It turns out, fatigue often sets in after an adrenaline rush, and getting shot at definitely caused my adrenaline to flow. The smell of coffee greeted me as my eyes fluttered open, and I took in the coffee mug sitting next to me on the nightstand. I sat up and yawned.

"Morning, sleepyhead," Michael said as he poured his own cup of coffee. His dark hair was tousled to perfection, and his sparkling blue eyes were bright, despite the fact that he was still wearing pajamas. Meanwhile, I felt like a symphony was warming up in my head. You know, when musicians play random notes to tune their instruments and percussionists randomly crash the cymbals? It felt like that.

"How is it that I'm the one that came back early, and you're the one looking bright-eyed and bushy-tailed?" I asked, wiping the sleep out of my eyes.

"What can I say? It's a gift."

"Lucky." I reached over to pick up the coffee mug and inhaled its magical aroma.

"What happened to you last night, anyway?" Michael asked while getting fresh clothes out of the suitcase.

"Hm?" I asked.

"Your knees."

"Oh." I looked down under the sheet for the scrapes that had been there when I went to bed but now were healed. Smooth pink skin was all that remained.

"Couldn't let you bleed all over the hotel sheets now, could I? What type of boyfriend would I be?" Michael teased.

"Oh, well, aren't you sweet? It was nothing. I tripped walking back with Edith and took a tumble on the sidewalk. Not very ladylike, but I'm okay now —better than okay. Thank you. What time did you get in?"

"Oh, about midnight."

"And you're happy to be awake right now? What time is it anyway?"

"A bit after nine."

"No, it isn't." It felt more like seven. I rubbed my temples.

"Headache?"

"A bit. No thanks to you," I quipped.

"Hey, I ordered the tequila. The martini was all you."

"Don't remind me." I did like a good dirty martini, but I didn't usually chase it with a shot of tequila.

"And I healed your cuts and got you coffee," Michael pointed out.

"Okay, you're forgiven then. Now go get in the shower and get ready to do whatever it is you're supposed to be doing right now."

"Golf," Michael replied.

"Golf? You boys have it so easy."

Michael shrugged. "I know, terribly unfair," he smirked.

While Michael went to get ready, I tried to wake up. I closed my eyes and breathed in the morning caffeine once more. It was going to be a two-cups-of-coffee morning.

Unfortunately, the minute the caffeine kicked in, my sleepiness was replaced with anxiety. I tried not to have a panic attack as I sipped my coffee. I was one hundred percent feeling the time crunch. If I didn't solve this case soon, like today soon, I would have to convince Michael to stay in Chicago a couple of extra days, and I wasn't sure how I was going to do that. We could probably take in a Cubs game, but sooner or later, I would have to confess what was really going on. It was a conversation I didn't want to have.

I decided I would save any confession until after the wedding. Who knew? Maybe I'd get lucky and solve the case before then. Stranger things have happened.

After getting ready for the day, Michael headed out. They were hoping to get in eighteen holes at the club before the afternoon ceremony. I went to check on Mary, and on the walk over, I thought about how weddings were way less stressful for the groom. All they had to do was slip on a tux and say I do. If I ever got married, I'd like to skip the stress altogether. I wonder how Michael felt about eloping?

I stopped walking.

"Did I just think that?" I asked the deserted hall-way. I shook my head and started walking again, reminding myself it was only natural to think about marrying your boyfriend when you were at a wedding. And yet, I felt like it was something more. I definitely needed a witchy pow-wow with my besties sooner rather than later. Mariana, who I liked to think of as the "mom" of the group (just don't tell her that), would talk some sense into me or hit me upside the head. Both would be effective.

Thankfully, we had a debriefing session coming up soon. Twice a year, the Agency summoned all of us time-traveling witches for a long weekend away, where we reflected on our recent cases, shared our tips and tricks of the trade, and gelled together as a team. Think of it as a work conference with fruity cocktails and sand between your toes, or it would be if I had my way. Word on the street was management wanted to send us someplace snowy next time. Believe me, my boss would get a strongly worded email, or maybe a straight curse, from me if she pulled that.

I was rounding the corner toward Mary's suite when I heard a scream behind her door. Immediately I raced forward and began frantically knocking at the door.

"Mary! Mary, can you open the door?" I banged on the door a couple more times. "Mary! Are you okay?"

I looked up and down the hallway to see if there was someone I could ask for help before I came to my senses and placed my hand on the doorknob, ready to use my magic to unlock it. That was the problem thinking about Michael and marriage. It threw me off my game. The lock's internal pieces were clicking together when Ruthie opened the door from the other side. I skipped the formalities and walked in past her.

"What's going on? What's wrong?" I looked over to Mary. She was standing in front of the closet door, her face frozen in horror. My mind started to race, wondering what was in the closet, and I prayed it wasn't a dead body. Magic flooded my body and made my fingertips tingle. The hairs raised on my arms. My senses were on high alert, as was my power. Cautiously, I walked over, ready to defend myself if needed. I looked behind me. Ruthie stood at the open door, peering casually out into the hallway.

And then I was standing next to Mary, looking in the closet.

"What happened?" I asked after I found my voice.

"It's a tragedy!" Mary wailed.

"It's something," I commented. Someone had taken a pair of shears, or maybe it was just a machete and shredded Mary's wedding dress. Ribbons of white fabric and scraps of lace were all that remained of the once elegant dress as pieces dangled precariously from the white satin hanger. Dozens of pearl buttons littered the floor. Even the plastic covering that had housed the dress had been cut up. Strips of white plastic acted as a bed for the dress's remnants.

"My dress. My beautiful dress." Mary's lips barely moved. Her eyes locked straight ahead in shock. I had to admit the destruction was pretty impressive. It was as if someone had taken out every ounce of rage they had on the dress, slicing and dicing it into oblivion. Even the friendly mice from Cinderella would have a hard time putting that dress back together.

"Something's wrong with your dress?" Ruthie asked, still standing in the doorway.

"When's the last time you saw it in one piece?" I asked, stepping over and taking a closer look at the remnants.

"I don't know." Mary shook her head as if trying to think. "Yesterday? The day before? I don't know. I hung it up here in this closet, and I haven't had to come in here for anything. My other dresses are right here in this closet." Mary pointed to the second wardrobe.

Once again, my heart rate picked up as I put my hand on the second closet door handle. I didn't even want to guess what I'd find inside. I held my breath and tugged it open, but inside everything looked normal. Not a single thread was out of place on the rest of Mary's dresses. I let out my breath. Sooner or later, my luck was going to run out. It felt like it always did.

"What about you, Ruthie? Did you see anyone in here?" I asked, even though I had a feeling that it wouldn't be hard to pull one over on a sloth. I felt terrible for saying that, but it was the truth.

"No, I haven't seen anyone in here except Mary," she replied.

I motioned for Ruthie to come in and shut the door behind her. Then I led Mary over to the bed and sat beside her. Her hand trembled in my palm.

"What am I going to do? The wedding is in a few hours. I'm never going to be able to find a dress. Why is the entire world against Jim and me marrying?" Mary buried her face in her hands and began sobbing in earnest. I rubbed her back and tried to calm her.

"I understand you're upset, but it's just a dress—"

Mary cut me off. "You have to be kidding me, right?" She was hysterical and clearly wasn't the person who destroyed her wedding dress. Mary might've stood to gain from Mrs. Stein's death, and she obviously had issues with Xavier, but I couldn't pin everything on her. The way she was crying and carrying on tugged on my heartstrings.

"Hear me out. We're in Chicago. There are plenty of bridal boutiques here. We have enough time to find something for today, and let's be honest, Jim's crazy about you. He wouldn't care if you wore a trash bag." That got a snicker out of Ruthie.

Mary, for her part, looked up at me hopefully.

"I'm serious. Jim doesn't care what you wear as long as you still want to marry him—that's all that matters. Ruthie," I said, turning my attention to the sloth, "would you mind getting Mary some ice water?"

"Oh, yeah, sure. I guess so."

"Great, thanks." It took a couple of minutes, but eventually, Ruthie left us alone, and I decided to tell Mary that I had overheard her conversation with Xavier last night.

"Don't tell Jim, please don't tell Jim," Mary pleaded. "He has no idea I ever dated Xavier. It was before our time. I didn't even know they were childhood friends."

"I wasn't going to. My point is, maybe he's the person who destroyed your dress. Where did you go last night after the jazz club?"

Mary closed her eyes and shook her head. "Nowhere really. I walked around downtown, got a cup of coffee, and sat on a park bench. I just really needed to be outside and clear my head. I got back in my room sometime after eleven and went right to bed."

"That's it? Nothing else?"

"No." Mary shook her head. "Oh wait, I ran into Jim's mom too. I forgot about that."

"What?"

"She was getting back in at the same time I was. She said she felt restless and couldn't sleep. She thought a walk would help her, but personally, I think it takes more than fresh air to calm that woman down. Don't tell Jim I said that either."

When I assured her that I wouldn't, Mary continued. "It didn't work, though. Sally looked frazzled as ever. Her face was flushed, and she looked a mess. I felt bad for her."

I wasn't sure how I felt about Sally. Jim's mom was moving steadily up the suspect list. Again, not sure how she tied in with Jill Stein and Bernie Compton, but if Jim and Xavier were childhood friends, then surely she would know him.

But why shoot at me?

Unless she thinks I'm on to her. And in that case, she'd be right.

The knock on the door snapped me out of my thoughts. I assumed it was Ruthie returning with the ice water, but instead, I opened the door to find Mrs. Rigatti with her entourage, including a hairstylist and the delivery of a champagne brunch. I had planned to whisk Mary away for a mad dash shopping spree, but it looked like it would have to be a solo trip.

"Shut the closet!" Mary hissed. I did as Mary asked, locking the carnage inside. "I don't want my parents to know. Papa would probably use any excuse at this point to cancel the wedding."

"My lips are sealed."

"You look a mess, child. What did you do, stay up all night?" Mrs. Rigatti asked her daughter.

"Sorry, Mama. I had a hard time sleeping last night," Mary confessed.

"I should say so. Beatrice, set up over there," Mrs. Rigatti instructed the makeup artist. "You better get to work straight away."

I stood in front of Mary so that my back was to her mother, who was busy instructing the hired help. "Quick, tell me what the dress looked like. I mean, besides all the tulle and lace." I kept my voice low.

"Tea-length, white with layers of tulle. Lace overlay up top and for the long sleeves. I got it at Margaret's Bridal Salon a few blocks from here."

"I'm on it. Do you, by chance, know your size?"

"Oh, I know all my measurements by heart, here." Mary stood and fetched a pad of paper and a pen from the in-room desk and jotted her measurements down. "I measure myself every day, don't you?"

"Like clockwork," I lied, taking the folded-up paper from her hand.

"And take my charge card." Mary handed me her gold and blue striped BankAmericard. It was the same colors we would associate with Visa today. "I don't care how much it costs."

"Got it." I slipped the card into my pocket. "I'll meet you here as soon as possible. Don't worry about a thing." I patted Mary's hand and took off out the door.

FOURTEEN

Before leaving The Duke, I stopped by the front desk and asked for directions to Margaret's Bridal Salon. I didn't have time to wander all around downtown Chicago.

Thankfully, the clerk was able to find the shop in the phone book and provided me with the exact address. I wasted no time hopping in a cab. Well, that and I didn't want to get shot at again. I doubted the perpetrator would strike in broad daylight, but I wasn't taking any chances. However, as the taxi cruised past the Italian bakery from earlier in the weekend, my mouth fell open in shock.

"Stop the cab!"

The driver looked over his shoulder in alarm.

"Please. Can I get out here?" I asked again.

"Suit yourself, lady." The cab driver pulled over to the curb, and I hastily paid and exited the vehicle.

Standing on the sidewalk and being led to a squad car was Mrs. Lucci. A string of what I imagined to be insults in Italian were flowing out of the woman's mouth. Her hands would have punctuated the statements if they weren't handcuffed behind her back.

"Mama, please. Just go. I'll meet you there," her daughter, Rosa, said. But the old baker was not listening. Her actions could've been classified as resisting arrest with the way she twisted and hollered. Detective Randle might want to watch his shins.

A crowd started to form, made up of individuals from both inside and outside the bakery. Ladies in their fine dresses, complete with coordinating hats and matching gloves and pushing baby buggies, stopped and stared. As did older gentlemen with their hats and canes out for Saturday morning walks. The spectacle outside the bakery was a sight. It wasn't every day you saw an older Italian woman get arrested—especially one as feisty as Mrs. Lucci.

"Don't worry, Mama. I'll call your brothers. They'll know what to do," Rosa hollered as the detective managed to fold Mrs. Lucci into the back of the black-and-white squad car, but not before she got one swift kick in. Detective Randle swore under his breath.

"Don't kick!" Rosa shouted at her mother before the door shut. "And please stop talking," Rosa said to herself more than anyone. Behind the glass, Mrs. Lucci's lips were still moving, not taking an ounce of her daughter's advice.

"What's going on?" I asked Rosa.

Rosa slapped her hand on her heart. "Oh, you scared me. It's a nightmare. The detective showed up here this morning with a search warrant, and next thing I know, he's coming out of the back kitchen with a little bag full of white powder that he said was poison."

"They found poison in your kitchen?" I kept my voice low.

"That's what he said. I guess it matches whatever happened to Barbara Jean."

"She was poisoned? He knows that for a fact?"

"He must. He's arrested Mama for the crime."

"Are you kidding me? Your mother wouldn't poison anyone." Mrs. Lucci was more the type to put The Eye on you or some other old-world curse.

"That's what I told him, but he wouldn't listen to me. The detective said eyewitnesses saw Mama and Mary get into a fight, and then the next thing they knew, Mary's cake was poisoned."

"I'd hardly count that as a fight," I added.

"I know. I told Detective Randle that was Mama just being Mama." Rosa folded her arms. A worried expression settled onto her face.

"But how does Detective Randle even know the cake was poisoned? He didn't take a sample of it the day it happened."

"He didn't, but an officer did. One came back in and took the plate and everything." Rosa sighed in frustration. "You know, I really wanted the police to get to the bottom of this, but right now, it feels like is we've been set up."

I had to agree with Rosa. It all sounded highly convenient.

"Did the detective say what the poison was?" I asked.

"No, but it looked like sugar."

"Regular table sugar?"

"Mm-hm," Rosa confirmed. The squad car pulled away and left Rosa and me on the sidewalk. Without a scene, people began to disperse.

"Maybe you were set up. How hard would it be for someone to sneak into your kitchen and swap out the sugar with poison or even sprinkle a little bit of it on Mary's cake?"

"Not hard at all. Half the time I leave the back

door open because the kitchen gets so hot. Someone could easily walk in."

"And who was here working Thursday?"

"Just me and Mama. It's usually just the two of us on most days. My cousins help around the holidays."

We both thought for a moment.

"It just makes me sick to my stomach. I don't know what to do," Rosa added.

I looked behind me into the packed bakery, where people were looking around in shock, Edith Adams included. She was sitting at a front table, looking out at us, with a cappuccino on the table in front of her.

"Mama's bark is worse than her bite. She might run her mouth, but she would never poison anyone, especially not Vito Rigatti's daughter."

"I believe you. Listen, let me help you close things down here and then you can go to the police station and see if you can find out what's going on."

"It's okay. I'm going to call my uncles. Mama's brothers might be the only ones who can talk some sense into her." Rosa looked at the packed bakery. "You don't think everything's poisoned, do you?" Rosa's voice was practically a whisper.

"No, I think somebody targeted Mary Rigatti, but Barbara Jean took the fall by accident. It's been, what, two days and nothing else has happened?"

"Good point, but I'll still feel safer if I pull everything and start from scratch."

"I hear you."

We walked inside the bakery, and Rosa addressed her customers. "Due to an unexpected event, we're going to have to close the bakery for the rest of the day. If you could finish your purchases or come see me to take them to go, that would be wonderful." Rosa went behind the counter and set about her work, passing out to-go bags and cups.

I planned on joining her and lending a hand, but I first wanted to catch up with Edith. She looked somewhat worse for the wear. The jazz singer's usually curled locks were a mess, and her complexion was washed out, almost ashy.

"Are you okay?" I asked as I sat down.

"I had an awful night."

"Yeah, I know. Someone shot at us."

"No, after that."

"Something bad happened after that?"

"Yeah, if you can believe it."

"Wow, what happened?"

"Well, after I got home, I couldn't shake the feeling that someone was, you know, watching me." Edith leaned toward me over her cappuccino and kept her voice low.

"I hate that feeling," I remarked, thinking about a couple of restless nights I've had back on the farm.

"Me too. I can usually shake it, but not last night. I eventually fell asleep on the couch, but when I woke up to move to the bed, there was someone in my room."

"What!"

"They were crawling in through my window. I freaked and threw the first thing I could grab at them, a perfume bottle. It hit them in the face and cracked the window."

"Oh, my goodness. Are you okay?"

"I'm fine. They took off running after that, and I was too stunned to chase after them."

"Did you call the police?"

Edith nodded. "Nothing they could do by the time they got there. They told me to keep my doors and windows locked and call them if I saw anything suspicious."

"And you didn't see what the person looked like?"

"No. It was dark. I only had the hall light on, and their face was covered."

"Holy cats."

"Yeah. Now you see why I look like this." Edith circled her face with her finger and laughed.

I sat back and thought for a moment. "You know what that means?"

"Huh?" Edith asked over the rim of her mug.

"Whoever was shooting at us last night might've been aiming for you and not me." Edith and I both stared at each other. I continued my train of thought. "What if ... what if Bernie Compton wasn't the intended target? What if it was you?"

"What? Why me?"

"I don't know. Any enemies jump out from your memory?"

"Trust me, I've been thinking about that all night, and nothing comes up. I had an ex-boyfriend get a bit handsy, but last I knew, he was down in Georgia."

"No, but you are in with the Rigattis, and they seem to be the connection between all these cases. You know what? I think we need to go back to the crime scene."

"I think you're right."

Edith drank her cappuccino while I helped Rosa finish up with her customers. "I'm staying at The Duke. We have the wedding this afternoon, but if you need me, leave a message there, and I'll be sure to check in," I said to Rosa as the last customer walked out the door.

"Thank you, Vee," Rosa replied.

"And try not to worry. We'll get to the bottom of this. I know your mother's innocent, and somehow, I'll prove it."

Edith and I raced over to her apartment complex and headed straight downstairs to the laundry room.

"What's that?" Edith asked as we approached the room's door.

"Danger, Keep Out," I read the notice and then tugged on the door. Sure enough, it was locked. I could open it, but I wasn't sure that was the smartest move.

"Now, what do we do?" Edith asked.

"Let's go talk to management. Hopefully, whoever is working can give us some answers," I replied.

"Good idea. The office is this way." Edith led me back outside and over to the adjacent apartment building that mirrored the same one she lived in. They looked to be sister properties. When Edith opened the front door, I could immediately see the office to the left. It was as if the apartment company had foregone one of the apartments and turned it into an office.

"Hey, Kathy," Edith said to the middle-aged brunette behind the counter.

"Edith! So good of you to stop on by. You know, my husband and I caught your show last weekend at the Green Light. Fabulous as always."

"Aw, thanks. Always nice to hear that."

"And what a fright you had last night. My word. I would never imagine such a thing happening here."

"Thanks," Edith replied.

Before she could say another word, Kathy added, "I've already called in to have your window repaired, and I'm typing up a memo right now to all the residents. We need to keep our eyes out and stay safe. Let that bad man know he can't break in here again."

"I appreciate that. Listen, do you know what's going on with the laundry room? It says it says keep out," Edith asked.

"Oh yes, I'm afraid the laundry room has given us quite a few headaches lately," Kathy replied.

"What do you mean?" I interjected.

"Well, besides the unfortunate incident with Mr. Compton, other tenants have been complaining."

"About what exactly?" Edith asked.

"Oh, all sorts of things. Headaches, upset stomachs. Mrs. Martin said she got lightheaded after doing one load of whites. I've sent our maintenance man over after every complaint, and he can't find anything. I have no idea what could be to blame, but until I find out, I don't think it's a good idea for anyone to be down there. Sorry about that."

"No, that's okay. I think that's smart," Edith replied.

"You're more than welcome to use the units over

here. Keep in mind, though, it's almost impossible to catch an open machine," Kathy added.

"No, that's all right. Think I'll stick to the laundromat for now," Edith said.

"Mind if I take a look?" I asked Kathy.

"Oh, um—"

"I'm pretty good with appliances," I lied.

"Sure, I guess. Why not. Maybe you'll find something." Kathy opened her desk drawer, fetched out a gold key, and handed it over. "This will get you in. Please be careful and promise to bring the key back when you're done."

"Sure thing," I replied, plucking the key from Kathy's hand.

"What time is it?" I asked Edith as we hightailed it back to her apartment building and jogged downstairs.

"Almost eleven."

"Okay, we have to make this quick. I still need to get Mary a new wedding dress."

"Say what?"

"Long story. Let's hope this wasn't a waste of time." I stuck the key in the door and unlocked it. It would have been just as easy for me to break in, but I thought it was more polite to ask for the key, and it would help explain how we got in there if we did find anything.

The damp and dank basement gave me the chills. It must've done the same thing to Edith as she crossed her arms and rubbed her shoulders.

"Let's make this quick. This space gives me the heebie-jeebies. I'm never doing laundry down here again," she said.

"Agree." The sooner we got out of there, the better. The spider incident from the last time I was in that room was fresh in my mind. I brushed my shoulders off just in case.

Edith and I split up. She examined the dryers, and I checked out the washing machines. I looked behind the machines and tried not to freak out at the amount of dust and cobwebs that zigzagged across the hoses and electrical cords.

"Yuck," I said.

"What? What did you find?" Edith asked from over by the dryers.

"Only cobwebs," I said, peering into one machine's drum.

"What about carbon monoxide poisoning?" Edith asked from the dryer. "Look at this."

I walked over and looked behind the dryer Edith was standing next to.

"Someone's disconnected the vent. Look, the duct is missing," she said.

"You're right."

"Do you think that would do it?" Edith asked.

"Yeah, except there's only one problem. These dryers are electric." There was only one plug behind the dryer as opposed to a plug and a gas valve connection.

"Well, phooey." Edith sighed.

I opened the dryer and peered in. "Wait, what's that?"

It was hard to make out details in the dim light, but I might have found our smoking gun. I surveyed the room and found what I was looking for on the windowsill. I tried not to cringe as I removed the flashlight and blew off the cobwebs. My friend, Mr. Eight Legs, scurried into the corner. I let the spider be, and with one quick switch, the flashlight clicked on, and I was able to shine the light directly into the dryer.

"What do you think that is?" I asked Edith as the light shone on the white residue around the dryer drum. Edith bent closer and stuck her head in to take a better look.

Instinctively, I used my hand to pull her back. "I don't think that's a good idea. Whatever it is, I bet that's what's making people sick."

"You think it's poison?"

"I do, and the fact that the dryer vent is disconnected would ensure it would stay in the room." I stood there and thought for a minute. "Do you always do your laundry on Tuesdays?"

"Usually. It's the band's day off. So, a perfect day for laundry."

"Well, if you were the intended target, don't you think it would make it pretty convenient to go after you when you were downstairs here?"

"Now you're freaking me out."

"Sorry. I forget not everyone's used to having a target on their back."

Edith seemed to look at me in a new light. "What is it that you do exactly?"

"Like I said, I'm a private investigator ... of the supernatural sort." I left off the part about being a time traveler. Revealing that secret was always against the rules, even if you were talking to an up-and-coming famous jazz musician. "Listen, let's run over and tell Kathy what we suspect, and she can call the police. I'm not sure if it will help Mrs. Lucci or not, but hopefully, she doesn't have any connections to anyone in this building, and it will encourage the police to look elsewhere."

"Okay, that sounds like a good plan. Then what?"

"Then you and I are going to run down to Margaret's Bridal Salon and pick out a new wedding dress for Mary, and together we will make our way over to The Duke."

Edith opened her mouth to object but quickly closed it.

"I want you by my side. I can't protect you if you're not with me, got it?" I said.

"Got it. Just let me run into my apartment and get changed."

"If you want, I can also use some glamour to freshen up your look." I hoped my offer didn't offend Edith, but she looked rough.

"Oh, girl, that would be a godsend."

"Okay, let's go."

FIFTEEN

"Hey, where do you think I could go to find a copy of Nancy's newspaper?" I was standing in Edith's kitchen while she gathered her wardrobe for the reception. The space was dated for the period with its black linoleum countertops, butter yellow tiled backsplash, and peeling floral wallpaper. The painted white cabinet drawers didn't fully shut, and the appliances gave me pause.

I eyed the stove with curiosity and thought of a good topic to cover at the next debriefing session—historical appliances. You think all stoves work the same until you're thrown back in time and find yourself staring at a six-burner beauty. While we're at it, we should probably cover cooking. Nothing is worse than getting blasted to the past and expected to be a housekeeper. No amount of my magic can conjure up meatloaf. Believe me, I've tried. I was not a kitchen witch.

"Who's Nancy?" Edith stuck her head out of her room.

"Sorry, I forget that not everyone knows her. She's the editor of the Midnight Express. It's a supernatural daily."

"Oh, the Midnight Express I've heard of. Where to get it, though? Let me think. Most people have it delivered to their house, but there's a newspaper stand off Monroe that would carry it. An old shifter runs it, or you know what, Merle's probably has it."

"Who's Merle?"

"It's the storefront for Merlin's Magical Emporium. It looks like a dump from the outside, but that's just a charm."

"Is it close by?"

"Uh-huh. A couple blocks off Michigan and honestly not far from the bridal shop."

"Perfect." If Merle's didn't have what I was looking for, then I could always ask Nancy at the wedding. This case had far too many suspects. It was time to start narrowing them down, and maybe the newspaper article or photos held the clues. "You about ready?"

Edith came out of her room dressed to perfection.

She wore an off-the-shoulder swing dress in a rich wine color. The hue helped bring her complexion back to life. She painted her lips in a coordinating shade. Dark coal lined her eyes, matching the heels on her feet. I felt woefully underdressed.

"You don't need any magic. You look beautiful," I remarked.

Edith laughed. "Ha, this little old thing? Actually, who am I kidding? It's new. Sales rack at Bonwit Teller. Isn't that store perfection?"

"That it is. Are you ready, then?" I asked.

"Let's do this."

The outside of Merle's looked like a washed-up record store. Vinyl records hung from fishing line in the dusty window display or make that parts of records. Some were cracked, and only slivers were left dangling. The remaining pieces lay broken on the ground. Record players, which looked like boxy leather briefcases, were propped open on elevated stands and tilted forward for window shoppers. Well, two were tilted forward. One had fallen off the stand and was on the display floor along with the broken records. The storefront sign at one time read Merle's, but now all that was left was the "Mer" and an apostrophe. The rest of the banner had faded over time, and Merlin had never bothered to replace it, or rather, that's what the store's magical charm wanted you to believe.

Edith opened the shop's door, and we stepped inside. The small narrow space was only wide enough to have one aisle that ran down the middle of it. It comprised folding tables with bins placed on top stuffed with records. The yellow tiled floor was cracked, and dust bunnies peeked out from under the tables. An older gentleman with Coke-bottle glasses was reading the newspaper and greeted us when we walked in.

"Good morning, ladies, or is it afternoon now?" He put down the paper and peered down his long nose at his wristwatch, revealing a T-shirt that read "Vote for Kennedy" and an unruly sparse of thin, white hair. He was standing behind a counter with two built-in record players. The turntables were screwed directly onto the table. One freely spun the man's coffee cup around, which didn't seem to bother him one bit. On the front of the counter was something that looked like an old telephone receiver minus the speaking part. All that remained was the piece you'd hold up to your ear with a black cord connected to it. My guess was that it was to sample the records, or that's how it should work if the cables were actually plugged in. I looked down and saw the connecting jack on the floor, clearly not plugged in.

"Hey, you don't by chance have a copy of the Midnight Express here, do you?" I asked.

"I do. It's right downstairs." The man pointed directly over my shoulder, and I turned and saw a set of stairs magically appear going down to the basement. As in, they developed right before my eyes. I'd take a set of supernatural stairs any day over having to flush myself in or get dropped in through a phone booth. A hidden staircase was rather mundane given the alternatives available, but I wasn't about to complain. We were on a time crunch.

"Right. Thanks," I replied as if I already knew the stairs were there.

Edith was already two steps down. I hurried to catch up with her and made my way down the stairs. The lower level of the store was surprisingly busy. A dozen shoppers mulled around, picking up candles and smelling them before adding them to their shopping basket or holding various crystals and gems up to the shop's lighting as they inspected them for quality. Sales associates dressed in black slacks with white dress shirts and gold bow ties rang customers up and helped guests reach merchandise on the higher shelves, like eye of newt and vampire fangs—the type of items you didn't want the youngsters to get their hands on.

"Here's the paper," Edith said, walking toward

the checkout counter. Set off to the side next to the Round Up candy cigarettes, Chuckles jelly candy, coconut Long Boys, and Rocky Road candy bars were the supernatural newspapers.

I stopped mid-stride. "There's more than one of them?"

"Oh yeah. You have Twilight Times, the Supes Daily ... I think there's at least one other one."

"Who knew?" The newspapers were laid out like supermarket tabloids with a similar layout and head-lines, only the supernatural stories were real. I'm sure the look was intentional. If anyone mundane ever came across one, they'd think it was a regular super-market tabloid.

I picked up the Supes Daily. The headline read "Unicorn Hair Shortage. Wand Makers Panicking." Below the fold were two other articles, one about a shifter cat burglar and "Goblins, Can You Trust Them?" The rest of the paper was full of similar arti-cles and community events, and nothing about the "Scared to Death" cases. I would skip the Twilight Times and go straight to Nancy's paper, but a Times article caught my attention: "Poison, Can You Smell It?"

I picked the paper up and began reading the article.

After a series of suspicious attacks in the Grove

Park neighborhood along Northern Michigan Avenue, we decided to put people's noses to the test. According to inside sources, the recent attacks, all targeting members of the supernatural community, are believed to be caused by potassium cyanide, and not a curse or ghost as some other newspapers have reported. This colorless crystal-like salt, similar in appearance to sugar, is highly soluble in water, producing hydrogen cyanide, which smells like bitter almonds. The poison affects individuals immediately, causing victims to pass out and often leading to death.

So, can you smell it?

It turns out it's a genetic trait, meaning some people, mundanes included, can naturally smell the poison. Also, as expected, shifters with a keen sense of smell can often pick up the distinct odor, as was the case here. A shifter on the Chicago PD forensic team discerned the scent of one of the victims and reported it to his supervisor, who was able to match it to evidence collected at the scene of the crime.

"The cake," I said.

As a reminder, never accept sweets or treats from strangers unless it's Halloween, and in that case, maybe bring a shifter along and have them sniff your haul. These are different times, Dear Reader. Stay safe.

"So, Barbara Jean was poisoned by the cake," I

said to Edith while I tried to talk the case out. "And Bernie from the dryer."

"But how?" Edith asked, not following.

"Look here. The article says cyanide is soluble in water, which means it dissolves in water, turning into hydrogen cyanide." And that was a poison I was familiar with, given its role in history with gas chambers. "If the murderer put the crystals in the dryer, and Mr. Compton added wet clothes ... it wouldn't take much to create the poisonous gas."

"And the vent was disconnected," Edith added.

"Right. So, the fumes stayed downstairs."

Edith visibly swallowed.

"Are you okay?" I asked.

"I can't believe someone wants me dead like that, and Mr. Compton? He wasn't a nice guy, but he didn't deserve what happened to him. It was supposed to be me. How am I supposed to wrap my head around that? And the guilt? I just don't know."

I put the paper down and pulled Edith off to the side. "Listen, this is not your fault. It's the killer's fault. You might not be the target."

"But you think I am."

I agreed that it was a strong possibility but not guaranteed.

Edith diverted her attention to the various bulk jars full of crushed and dried herbs.

"I don't know what I did to send someone over the edge like that, but there must be something." Edith sounded defeated.

"Don't worry, we'll figure that out. In the meantime—" My words failed me. Standing at the counter not more than ten feet away was Jim's mom, and she was sporting an impressive black eye. Sally looked over her shoulder, and I tugged Edith by the arm, so we both turned our backs to her.

"What? What is it?" Edith asked.

"Shhhh." I gestured with my head for Edith to follow me down the aisle, and the two of us hid behind a bookshelf. I peered around the books and tried to eavesdrop on Sally's conversation.

"Walked right into the doorframe. I don't know what's the matter with me these days," she said. "Anyway, you don't by chance have any powdered dragon's claw in, do you? Or a whole claw. I suppose I could powder it myself, but I'm a little pressed for time."

"Sure do. How much do you need?" the sales associate asked.

"Oh, a pinch or two should do the trick." Sally took her billfold out of her purse, and Edith and I slinked further back.

"Who is that woman?" Edith asked. "She looks vaguely familiar."

"That's Jim's mom, Sally. Michael told me she's a potions master."

"Hence the powdered dragon's claw."

"Right. But she also doesn't want Jim marrying Mary."

"What? Why not?"

"From what I gather, it has to do with Jim's brother. His marriage has put a rift in the family, and Sally's afraid the same thing might happen with Jim. Well that, and Antonia Rigatti leaves something to be desired. But, the point is she has a black eye! Did you say you smacked your intruder with a perfume bottle?"

"Hard enough to crack the window."

"*And* Sally's a witch, so she could've put a spell on the gun to silence it last night."

"You think it was her?" Edith pulled away from me and looked like she was about to give Sally a piece of her mind.

I yanked her back by the arm. "Don't say anything. I don't know for sure. Right now, it's only speculation. We need evidence."

"Oh, I'll give you some evidence, all right."

"I'm serious. I have no idea why she'd target you or Jill Stein or even Xavier for that matter, but I know she knows who Xavier is, given he's a childhood friend of Jim's."

"I'm only following about half of this," Edith confessed.

"Sorry." I sighed in frustration as I continued to watch Sally check out.

"You're just going to let her leave?"

"For now. I don't want her to know that we're on to her. Can you keep an eye on her during the wedding? Afterward, I can call in backup to help me search for evidence." By backup, I meant telling Michael what was going on.

Edith nodded. "Good. Now let's grab us a wedding dress and get back to Mary."

We left Merle's and ran over to Margaret's Bridal Salon. The inside of the boutique was painted wall to wall in the lightest shade of pink, with the carpeting being a deep teal, which surprisingly set off the row and rows of wedding dresses quite nicely. The store attendants wore dark gray dresses with three-quarter-length sleeves, belted at the waist, and fashioned with oversized buttons that ran up the front. The associates completed the look with oversized pink-chiffon neck bows.

We approached the front counter, where I explained the situation but got nowhere fast.

"I'm sorry, ma'am, like I said, Miss Rigatti's dress was one of a kind. I have nothing like it in the shop."

The perky blonde sales associate held up her empty hands.

I swished my head from side to side. There looked to be at least twenty dresses that were ankle length with lace, and that was only what was in my line of sight.

"Right, I understand that. We just need to find something comparable. It doesn't have to be perfect," I explained.

"The lace was handmade," the associate replied.

"Yes, and right now, any lace will do. Trust me," I insisted.

"And the tulle was the softest I've ever felt," the associate continued.

"Any tulle will do," I countered.

"The hours spent altering that dress. It was a masterpiece."

"Yes, and now it's trash. So, if you could help us find a new one, that would be great," I said.

"If you're certain ..." the associate trailed off.

"Quite," I replied.

"Oh, well, in that case, do you have an appointment?" The woman looked at us expectantly.

"Listen, lady, we don't have time for an appointment. What part of 'emergency' don't you understand?" Edith said, losing her temper. I felt the same way but managed to tuck my emotions in.

"How about we have a quick look around and see what we can find?" I raised my eyebrows, daring the associate to say something else. "Come on." I pulled Edith away from the counter.

"That woman is getting on my last nerve," Edith said through pursed lips.

"Mine too. Let's just find a dress and get out of here." Edith and I split up in a divide-and-conquer fashion.

I had two options at this point: dash around the store like a madwoman, trying to locate the perfect dress, or let magic do the heavy lifting. I bet you can guess which one I chose.

I found a quiet corner in the back of the shop at the end of one of the rows. It was away from the fitting rooms and the bustling attendants. I needed a quiet spot to help center myself and unlock my power. Facing a row of dresses, I closed my eyes and reached forward with my right hand, taking hold of one of the bagged dresses. I pinched the material between my index finger and thumb. I could feel the lace indentations underneath the clear protective plastic. In my mind, I pictured Mary walking down the aisle in a beautiful white lace dress. Her blonde hair was curled under, and her veil was held in place with decorative pearl combs. The same miniature pearls decorated the satin wrapped around her yellow-rose bouquet and matched the larger pearls on her necklace and bracelet.

"I needed to find this image or something better," I told the universe before saying these magical words:

What was destroyed must now be found,
As my magic circles round.

Whether you are hidden far or near,
I call you now to come meet me here.

I repeated the words three times and opened my eyes. I then looked around the salon and waited to be guided. My feet suddenly had a mind of their own. I felt pulled forward, walking without a clue as to where I was going. My feet carried me straight toward the front door.

"Edith, let's roll," I hollered over my shoulder, willing my feet to wait up even though they didn't want to.

"What?" Edith said, her hand holding up one of the gowns as she inspected it through the plastic.

"Come on," I nodded out the door. "We need to go!"

Edith quickly replaced the dress and hurried over to join me at the door.

"What's going on? Did you find a dress?" she asked.

"Not exactly. I cast a spell, and it is leading us to the dress."

"Oh." The two of us power-walked down the sidewalk, Edith keeping up like a champ in her high heels. "Any idea how far away this dress is?" she asked as we hoofed it.

"It shouldn't be far at all. When I said the spell, I assumed the dress was in the shop, but I guess another one has to be close by."

"Could your spell maybe tell us if we should take a cab?" Edith asked, half-joking.

I came to a screeching halt and turned my head to the left. "Bonwit Teller. Do they sell wedding dresses?"

"Well yeah, they have a bridal department."

"Then that's where we're supposed to be. I can feel it."

We swung in through the revolving door, bypassed the makeup and handbags, skipped the sensual experiences, and headed directly for the elevators.

"Which floor, miss?" The elevator operator asked.

"Bridal, please," I replied.

"Yes, ma'am," the man said. The elevator rose up to the third floor, at which time the operator announced, "Third floor, bridal department. Enjoy your shopping."

"Thank you so much," Edith and I remarked as we stepped off the elevator.

"Now, which way?" Edith asked me.

"This way," I said, feeling the pull of the dress on my solar plexus.

"Excuse me, how may we help you?" a sales associate asked us.

I held up my finger. "We only need to look around for a minute."

"Oh. I suppose that's all right," the woman replied, unsure of herself. She trailed along after us, her heels clicking on the floor, mirroring Edith's.

"So, when's the big day?" she asked as she struggled to keep up with us.

"Today," Edith replied flatly.

The woman opened and closed her mouth like a fish out of water.

We didn't try to explain what we were doing. Instead, I let my intuition guide us as we hooked a right, walked down an aisle of dresses, turned left, passed in front of a wall of mirrors, and took another left. I came to a stop.

"That's it. It's perfect." I said to the display in front of us.

"It's yellow," Edith remarked, scrunching her nose.

"Only the tulle and sash are yellow. The rest is white, and Mary loves yellow. Trust me."

Edith scrunched her nose. "I don't know."

"It's perfect. Always trust your intuition," I told Edith before turning to the associate. "We'll take this one."

"Take it?" she asked.

"Buy it. I'll buy this dress, and we need to move quickly. The wedding will be starting soon," I said.

"Wouldn't you like to try it on?" the associate asked.

"Oh no, the bride's not here."

The associate looked at me like I was crazy, but I couldn't help that.

"Should I just take this one?" I asked, and Edith was already unzipping the dress and tugging it off the mannequin's head.

Finally, the woman came to her senses. "Here, let me do that for you."

Edith and I stepped back. "Thank you."

SIXTEEN

"Is that the dress? Oh my goodness, it's perfect!" Mary squealed.

Antonia Rigatti looked less than impressed. "Whose dress?" She eyed the material through the garment bag.

"It's my dress, Mother," Mary replied with the same fierceness to her voice she'd used with Xavier the night before. She meant business.

"That is not your dress. I know what your dress looks like, and it certainly wasn't yellow." Antonia looked disgusted.

"No, it wasn't, but it should have been. I hate white. You know that. Papa knows that. And yet everyone insisted that I wear a white dress. But this?" Mary unzipped the garment bag so she could see the dress more clearly. "This is my dream dress. However did you find it?" Mary asked.

"It was magic," I replied with a smile.

"We have *you* to blame for this?" Antonia asked, turning her icy glare toward me.

I wanted to snap back to Antonia and say whoever shredded Mary's dress was to blame and that I had merely solved the problem, but I knew Mary didn't want her mother to know the details.

It was Mary who spoke up. "No, you have Vee to thank for this." Mary looked at me with happy tears in her eyes. "I don't know if I'll ever be able to repay you. You've saved my wedding time and time again. I owe you so much. I'll be forever grateful."

There was a knock on the suite door, and Edith, standing closest to it, opened it. On the other side was Adam the aardvark looking rather spiffy in a black tux with tails, along with Nancy, her camera in tow.

"Don't you look dreamy," Ruthie said, staring at her beau with adoration. Adam tugged on the suit coat and tilted his head from side to side as if he found the entire ensemble a bit restrictive.

Then he spotted Edith. "Aaaay, the jazz singer. I like your style." Adam pretended to play the trumpet. Complete with sound effects.

"Oh, thanks so much," Edith said, stepping aside

for Adam and Nancy to walk in the rest of the way and then looked at me with wide eyes as if asking, "Is he all right?"

"You get used to it," I whispered to Edith as she joined me.

"Jim asked Adam to fill in for Frank," Mary explained. "So now the wedding party is equal again."

"Oh, awesome. Should we get you in your dress then?" I asked Mary, not meeting Antonia's eyes.

"Yes, let's!" Mary exclaimed.

Nancy clicked away, taking pictures of Mary as she put on the finishing touches of her wedding attire. Iconic photos, like Antonia fastening her daughter's pearl necklace and clipping her veil in place. Mary made the perfect bride. She looked beautiful and was full of happiness. You could feel it just looking at her.

On the other hand, I needed a little bit of work, but after a bit of bibbidi bobbidi booing and a quick wardrobe change, I was ready to go, too. Michael and Jim were already at the venue, having arranged to shower and dress on site after their round of golf. All that was left was for the four of us—me, Mary, Ruthie, and Adam—to take the limo to the country club. Mary was more than willing to let Edith tag along in luxury, but she insisted on taking a cab with Nancy, and we couldn't talk her out of it.

The black Cadillac limo out front was a sight to behold. The behemoth beauty looked sharp, much like the twin tail fins in the back. The chauffeur opened the back door, revealing a cream leather interior with tan carpeting and matching footrests. It was as if a comfortable leather couch had been placed in the back of a car. The fifth seat was folded up and tucked into the back of the driver's seat in order for us to enter. The three ladies took the plush bench seat while Adam unfolded the second bench and sat there. The entire interior had chrome accents, including the analog clock and ashtrays built into the back of the driver's bench seat.

"This is some car," said Ruthie, mouth open in awe.

"It is pretty amazing," I said, feeling the plush seat beneath my bottom. "A woman could get used to this."

"And I'm getting married!" Mary squealed with happiness and clapped her hands in excitement.

Adam cupped his hands over his ears and hunched his shoulders, looking to Mary as if she'd lost her mind.

Before pulling away, a member of the hotel's concierge appeared with a tray of champagne glasses and passed each one of us a drink.

"I can't believe this is finally happening. I swear I

could just die of happiness." Mary put the champagne to her lips before pulling the glass away.

"What's wrong?" I asked.

"I don't know. It doesn't smell right." Mary scrunched her nose.

"Don't drink it!" I exclaimed.

Ruthie startled. "I wasn't going to drink the champagne anyway. I don't even like it," she commented.

I rolled the window down, taking everyone's glass and dumping them out one by one in the street. I wasn't taking any chances.

"You think it's poisoned?" Mary asked.

"Do you want to chance it?" I replied.

"That's messed up," Adam commented.

"Let's just be safe for now," I added.

"This has to stop," Mary said, getting emotional.

I pulled a tissue out of my purse. I was well stocked up for the afternoon. "I know. Believe me, I know."

I was pleasantly surprised when we got to the venue with how packed it was. I thought some of the guests would flake out given the pre-wedding brawl, but both sides of the family showed in full force. Although that didn't mean they wanted to be there. I had hoped that the outdoor venue would help dissipate some of the energy, but no such luck. The moment I stepped foot out of the limo, I could feel it.

I hated to say it, but the atmosphere felt toxic, leaving my magic on edge.

I exhaled a shaky breath. Regardless of how I felt, the stage was set, and it was showtime.

Mr. Rigatti met us at the limo. He took his daughter's hand and helped her out while a woman from the country club handed Mary her flowers. It was a simple yellow rose bouquet with pearl accents, like the one I had visualized in my spell.

"You look beautiful," Mr. Rigatti said, kissing his daughter's cheek.

Up ahead at the top of the stone steps was Nancy, capturing the once-in-a-lifetime moment. She was clicking away, and beside her was Alice, Jill Stein's best friend. The woman moved to tuck a piece of loose hair behind Nancy's ear, and Nancy swatted her hand away.

"I'm working, Mama, please stop," Nancy snapped. But Alice kept right on fussing.

"Just fix your hair. It's a mess," Alice said.

"Trust me, Mama, no one cares about me," Nancy remarked.

"And whose fault is that?" Alice quipped and then looked at me.

I shut my mouth and looked away. I had no idea Alice was Nancy's mother. Hopefully, Alice wouldn't make the connection with me. Maybe after the wedding, it wouldn't matter. In fact, Alice would probably be happy to know that I was looking into Jill's death.

Up ahead, the stone patio looked even more perfect than yesterday.

Guests filled each and every chair. Staff had tied bunches of baby's breath and miniature yellow roses to the chairs at the end of each row. A white runner lined the aisle way. And standing at the altar was Michael. Well, in between Jim and Adam. The groomsmen had each escorted a senior member of the family up the aisle and took their spot at the front, waiting for the ceremony to begin.

And then it was time for us to join them. Ruthie led the procession, sauntering up the runner while Edith sang Ave Maria acapella. I stood at the foot of the aisle, wishing Ruthie would pick up the pace ever so slightly. The longer I stood there waiting for my turn, the harder my heart began to beat in my chest.

The next thing I knew, it was my turn, and I was walking down the aisle toward Michael. My heart, which was thudding in my chest moments before, calmed down, and for a moment, I wished we were the ones getting married. The feeling was so overwhelming that I almost stopped moving, but thankfully my senses prevailed, and I continued walking.

At the end of the aisle, I smiled at Michael before veering off to the left.

Then it was Mary's turn. The bride cried happy tears as her father walked her down the aisle. I looked at Jim and saw him beam with pride, tears spilling out of his eyes. There was no question that he loved Mary, and she, him.

As the ceremony progressed, my mind finally had a moment to work out the case. I scanned the crowd. Sitting in the front row were Michael's parents, Sally and Stan. The powdered dragon's claw must have worked. The mother of the groom's face was flawless, but the woman still looked uncomfortable. She kept fidgeting with her purse. Opening and closing the metal snap, her eyes lost in space. Edith stood off to the side, her eyes glued to the woman.

Then I spotted Alice, sitting in the back row.

What if Jill Stein's best friend was the murderer? Could she have wanted her best friend's money for something else? But what? I looked over to where Nancy was still taking photographs. Could it be her daughter's newspaper? I remembered Alice commenting that Jill was fond of supporting hopeless cases. Perhaps, she wanted Jill to help her daughter's newspaper and killed her when she didn't? It was a stretch, I admit, but I needed to consider the possibility.

I looked over at Alice. She kept looking at her daughter and then back at Jim. Her expression was full of disappointment. My thoughts suddenly shifted as I took in the woman's expression. I could read her thoughts plain as day, and I wasn't a mind reader. She was thinking that it should be her daughter up there getting married. That would explain why she kept trying to kill Mary. She wanted to get rid of the bride. And what about Xavier? How did he wrong her? Perhaps he had slighted Nancy as well. Because they were childhood friends—

I didn't get to finish my thought because at that moment, Mary turned and handed me her bouquet as she and Jim were about to exchange their vows. Michael smiled at me over Jim's shoulder and met my look with a wink. The gesture sent butterflies dancing in my stomach. I turned and looked off in the distance. My mind was caught up in the case, and my emotions were running high when I heard the telltale click of a gun.

"Watch out!" I pushed Mary to the side toward the priest as a bullet grazed my shoulder. "Get down!" I shouted and wheeled around. My shoulder stung. The pain caused my magic to erupt. I felt the electricity sizzle and crack at my fingertips. Everyone hit the deck except for Michael. He ran after me as I tore through the crowd, Alice in my sights. I sent a blast of electricity, but the orb went wide and crashed into the clubhouse's glass window, shattering it. Alice covered her face with her arms as the glass rained down and used her back to push open the clubhouse's main door. Once inside, Alice went into an all-out sprint. Not watching where she was going, she crashed into a waitress, spinning her around and sending highballs flying. Alice didn't break her stride. I couldn't let her get away.

I charged forward and dove without thinking, catching Alice around the legs. It was an all-star tackle. We landed hard on the polished stone floor, and when the woman rolled over and attempted to flee, I saw that it was not Alice but her daughter Nancy.

"You've got to be kidding me," I said on the exhale as Michael apprehended her. Thankfully the country club employed security, and they were able to lend a hand with securing Nancy in handcuffs.

"He was supposed to marry me! He promised! We were five years old, and I said yes!" Nancy was wild out of her mind as the guard placed the cuffs around her wrists. "I've loved Jim since before I knew what love was."

"So, you tried to kill Mary," I surmised.

"Why wouldn't she eat the cake? What in the

world is the matter with a woman that won't even sample chocolate cake?" Nancy asked.

"Nancy!" Alice shouted in disbelief.

"Can it, Mother. Maybe if you hadn't pressured me every day of my life, I wouldn't be so desperate," Nancy snapped.

Alice stood in shock, not knowing what to say.

"And Jill? She wouldn't fund your newspaper, would she?" I said.

"No, not Jill." Alice slunk toward the floor. Thankfully, Mr. Rigatti caught her.

"It's your fault!" Nancy hollered at her mother. "My life was perfect until you met the Rigattis, and Jim met Mary. Not only did she break Xavier's heart, but now she's stolen Jim from me."

Alice didn't know what to say. I think she was in shock.

"When you couldn't get your own best friend to give me a thousand dollars, out of the millions she had, to get my paper running, that was the last straw. I had to take matters into my own hands," Nancy continued. "Jill deserved what she got—a sensational story." Nancy smiled wickedly.

More of the puzzle clicked into place.

"You created the news. Edith's death was supposed to make a good headline, too, wasn't it?" I was right. The up-and-coming starlet was the original intended target. Mr. Compton was just in the wrong place at the wrong time.

Nancy looked at the ground. She couldn't deny it.

"But why target Xavier?" I asked.

"Xavier was too smart for his own good. He passed through town and heard Mary was getting married. Started nosing around my business. He needed to go."

"What did you do, poison his water bottle? Sprinkle cyanide in the sauna?"

Nancy didn't answer me, but it didn't matter. The police would have enough to lock her away for a long time. Thankfully it didn't take them long to arrive and haul her away.

"Here, let me take care of that for you," Michael said, looking at my arm.

"How much damage is there?" I asked.

"It's not too bad. It'll be sore for a couple of days."

"I meant with the mundanes. How many of them saw my orb?" I replied.

"Always the job," Michael teased.

"I better get this called into the Clean-Up Crew." The crew was the Agency's supernatural scene cleaners. They did the dirty work.

"Son of a gun," I hissed as Michael worked his magic on my wound.

"Ssshh, give me a minute." Michael began chanting under his breath, and my skin grew cool under his touch. The pain wasn't gone completely, but my shoulder grew numb like I was given a shot of Novocain.

"Better?" Michael asked.

"Yes. Much."

Michael and I rejoined the wedding, where Jim was trying to console Mary.

"You took a bullet for me. I can't believe you did that," Mary said, wrapping me in a bear hug.

"Ow," I replied.

"Oh, my goodness. I'm so sorry!" Mary jumped back.

"It's okay. Michael worked on it a bit," I replied.

"You got some girl there, Michael," Jim said, clapping his best man on the shoulder.

"I know," Michael replied.

"So, where were we?" I asked.

"Are you sure you want to keep going?" Mary asked.

"You still want to get married, don't you?" I replied.

"Absolutely!" Mary replied enthusiastically.

It took a few minutes to regain order. It would've been quicker if Mr. Rigatti could've shifted into his lion form, but the guests came back together soon enough, and the wedding was able to continue.

"You're a friend of the family now, you hear me?" Mr. Rigatti said to me after the ceremony.

"Oh, thanks so much, sir. I appreciate it." I wasn't sure what that meant exactly, but I figured it was better to be on the crime boss's good side than the alternative.

SEVENTEEN

Later that night, after the fanfare, first dances, and cutting of the cake, Michael and I finally had a moment to ourselves.

"Just so you know, I knew you were working a case this whole time," Michael said after swallowing a piece of wedding cake.

"What? You did not." I took a fork full of cake off Michael's plate and put it in my mouth. I had no idea what Mary was talking about. This vanilla cake was delicious. Rosa and Mrs. Lucci had outdone themselves. Hopefully, the elder baker was free from police custody by now.

"Did too. It's something about the way your nose twitches when you're working a case, or maybe it's the twinkle in your eye."

"Are you serious? Not about the twinkle, but you knew?"

"Mm-hm."

"Why didn't you say anything?" I was stunned.

"I figured if wanted me to know, you would've told me."

Ouch. Michael's comment stung, but I deserved it. "I did want to tell you, just so you know. I was going to tell you tonight."

"Because you needed more time?" Michael asked.

"Yes, but more than that. I wanted you working by my side."

"Is that a fact?"

"It is. I like working with you and would've brought you onboard earlier, but I didn't want to ruin your weekend. I know how hard you work, and you said you wanted a break. I wanted you to have one, too. You deserve it."

"I appreciate that, but I think there's more to the story."

"What do you mean?" I wasn't following.

Michael took me by the hand and looked directly into my eyes. I wanted to break contact and look away, but I was a big girl and didn't.

"I know you were nervous about going away this weekend."

"I was, um ... I ... it's just..." I was stammering like

a fool.

Michael talked over me. "If I'm pushing you too hard or if you need space, tell me because I'm crazy about you. I'll take you however I can get you. In fact, I love you." Michael took my hand in his.

I gulped. "You do?"

"It might be the death of me, but I do." Michael smiled broadly.

"Good. Because I love you too." The words tumbled out of my mouth. Michael seemed as surprised as I was at my declaration, but I knew it was true. I'd be lying if I said otherwise.

"That's nice to hear." Michael slowly leaned forward. Instinctively, I leaned in too. His lips brushed mine, and I might have actually sighed.

"It's official," I whispered after our kiss.

"What?"

"I've turned into a soft-hearted fool." I wrinkled my nose.

Michael chuckled. "Yes, but you're my fool."

"I suppose that's alright."

"But promise me." Michael turned the conversation serious once more. "If you ever need space or anything, tell me."

"I will, and I'm sorry for acting like an idiot. I wasn't thinking straight."

"It's okay. I forgive you."

"You do?" I replied playfully.

"Mm-hm. No hard feelings," Michael winked.

We sat there for a moment, content to watch Jim twirl Mary around the dance floor. The couple was the picture of pure wedded bliss. I couldn't help but wonder if someday that would be us.

"Care to dance?" Michael held out his hand, and I accepted it. The music slowed as the band switched gears, and Edith's sweet, one-of-a-kind voice filled the air.

And as Michael led me out to the dance floor, I decided that it didn't matter what the future held or even what year it was. All that mattered was the here and now, and I couldn't ask for anything more.

* * *

Want more? Vee's next mystery is Time Will Tell: **https://books2read.com/u/baGqqQ**

Stephanie Damore Complete Works
Mystic Inn Mysteries

. . .

Spirited Sweets Mysteries
Bittersweet Betrayal
Decadent Demise
Red Velvet Revenge
Sugared Suspect
Indulgent Injury

Witch In Time
Better Witch Next Time
Play for Time
Time Will Tell

Beauty Secrets Series
Makeup & Murder
Kiss & Makeup
Eyeliner & Alibis
Pedicures & Prejudice
Beauty & Bloodshed
Charm & Deception

A Drop Dead Famous Cozy Mystery
Mourning After

ABOUT THE AUTHOR

Stephanie Damore is a USA Today bestselling mystery author with a soft spot for magic and romance, too. She loves being on the beach, has a strong affinity for the color pink (especially in diamonds and champagne), and, not to brag, but chocolate and her are in a pretty serious relationship.

Her books are fun and fearless, and feature smart and sassy sleuths. If you love books with a dash of romance and twist of whodunit, you're going to love her work!

For information on new releases and fun giveaways, visit her Facebook group at https://www.facebook.com/stephdamoreauthor/

facebook.com/stephdamoreauthor

twitter.com/stephdamore

instagram.com/steph_damore_author

bookbub.com/profile/stephanie-damore